ON TO CHEYENNE

ON TO CHEYENNE

Tom Curry

GUNSMOKE

This hardback edition 2010
by BBC Audiobooks Ltd
by arrangement with
Golden West Literary Agency

ISBN 978 1 408 46269 0

British Library Cataloguing in Publication Data available.

Printed and bound in Great Britain by
CPI Antony Rowe, Chippenham and Eastbourne

CHAPTER I
The Almighty Pen

FRANK WARREN'S brown eyes shone with excitement, and he licked his lips. The startling story he was setting up for the Cheyenne *Times* was so much dynamite.

"This," he said to his employer, Paul Tate, editor of the frontier newspaper, "will blow Cheyenne wide open!"

Tate nodded his graying head. His bulldog jaw was set and he looked grave. He was an experienced frontier journalist, and he knew that dynamite sometimes explodes and kills the man who dares to handle it. He was twenty years older than Warren and he had crusaded in other Western settlements.

"I want a circulation, Frank," he said seriously, "but that isn't why I'm doing this. Whenever a new town springs up, thieves hurry to it to prey on decent folks, before law and order can be

5

established. It's the duty of the press to expose such men, arouse the public so they will know whom to fight. That's what a paper is for, in my opinion. We should not only give the news but we should stand for what's right."

Warren took in what his mentor said. He was learning the game from the bottom, and Tate was a fine teacher. For as far back as he could remember Frank has wanted to be a newspaperman, and it was Tate who finally had offered him his big chance. Tate had taught him how to gather news, how to evaluate it, and the technical part of newspaper work too —editing, the mechanics of getting out a weekly frontier newspaper, the laborious type-setting by hand, inking, proofing, operation of the hand press. The press had been brought to the railhead and then transported the rest of the way to Cheyenne by ox cart.

Warren was a tall young man with a shock of curly, dark hair, and a slender body which was clad in old blue shirt and overalls that were smudged with ink. He had studied for two years in an Eastern university, but the death of his father—his mother had died when he was a baby—had made it imperative that he earn his living. He had drifted West and Tate had picked him off the road the previous spring. He was a good-looking lad, but it had been the eagerness in his eyes which had attracted Tate. Warren still was eager, and had a boundless enthusiasm for the newspaper game.

6

Tate knew all the ropes. With him, experience took the place of youth's first tremendous flush of power. But Tate was able to enthuse, too, at times. The editor was aware of the great effect of the written word on mankind, and that a newspaper, to be successful, must do more than print cold facts.

There had been a number of crusading stories for which Tate was responsible, and some of his slogans, such as "Boom Cheyenne!" "Cheyenne, Biggest Little City West of the Missouri!" "Cheyenne for Territorial Capital!" "Make Wyoming a State!" "Let Cheyenne Show the Nation the Way!" had been universally adopted by the citizens of the settlement.

Tate sought to arouse civic pride among the get-rich-quick population sliding in and out of the settlement, and in those who made money from the trade. One of his ideas had been to interest people in using natural gas to illuminate the town street lamps; even for power and heating. "Let Cheyenne Be First to Light the Way—With Gas!" his paper had heralded.

OFTEN Tate's editorials sounded like royal pronouncements but they had authority and ideas behind them; they made men stop for a moment and think.

But Tate's other pet schemes had been relegated to the background by this story which he and young Warren were now preparing. It would blast Cheyenne out of her complacency if anything would. It ought to have national value, which would help put Cheyenne on the map.

Tate bit the end off a black Cuban cheroot, and began chewing on it, but did not light up. He wore a green eyeshade and was in his shirt sleeves which were held in place by faded pink sleeve garters.

Oil lamps hung from rusty chains attached to the rough beams, holding the little wooden building together, and insects came in at will to swarm about the lights. The acrid odor of printer's ink, newsprint paper and metal filled the office.

With tweezers Frank Warren had picked out the letters from the case with which to make the vital words of the hand-written script. After he had set them he had locked them in forms and inked them with a roller. Now they were in printed form.

"Read that first part of the story back to me again, Frank," ordered Tate.

Warren went and stood under the nearest lamp. His hands were discolored by ink and there was a smudge on his nose and over his eyebrow where he had impatiently swatted at mosquitoes. He began reading in a clear young voice the paragraph Tate wanted to hear read:

The criminal gangs infesting our fair city are headed by a man of the most evil reputation. Even on the frontier this individual would be shunned if his true nature were known. Outlaws flocked to

Cheyenne as soon as it became apparent that the Union Pacific intended making it an important stop. Criminals of every ilk—garroters, train robbers, road agents, lot jumpers, gunmen and deserters from both armies in the recent conflict—have made up a powerful combine which is preying on our honest elements.

Warren broke off as Tate gave a warning hiss.

"Oh—it's only your shadow!" said Tate, with relief, as a strange figure silently came in the open back door.

He was tall and his braided hair, black as ink, was shoulder length. His face was expressionless, his black eyes beady, his cheek-bones wide and high.

"Howdy, Johnny!" sang out Warren.

The Crow Indian, both men knew, was harmless—at least in town—and Warren had often given him money with which to buy food and drink. Johnny Three Snakes was the name he went by. He grunted, waiting there in his nondescript garments made from an old horse blanket, until Warren gave him a fifty-cent piece. The Crow turned then and left without a word. "Go on," said Tate to Warren.

The next paragraph, read:

Through perilous investigations this paper has ferreted out the facts of the situation and now sets them down for the public good. Among the first to hurry here to Cheyenne was the man we mean to name. He had been a political figure in St. Louis but at last had gone too far and the shameless crimes he had perpetrated were traced to him. He fled from

9

justice and, escaping in the night, reached the frontier.

Just ten months ago he came to Cheyenne and now he is master of the criminal outlaw element infesting the town. Understanding how to organize such bands, a past master at corruption and control of gunmen, this man formed his staff. They have taken over every profitable phase in Cheyenne—the crooked gambling, and the shady districts.

Some. serve as road agents or desperados. No crime may be committed within ten miles of this settlement unless the perpetrator pays his tribute to the boss. He has bands raiding trail herds which bring Texas cattle to Wyoming, and others specializing in robbing the thousands of workers on General Dodge's transcontinental railroad.

Warren paused, glancing up. He swallowed, licked his lips again. The noises of the settlement came clearly through the open windows, a raucous cacophony of mingled music, hoarse voices of men, the shrillness of women.

Down the street a cowboy in his cups was shooting his revolver.

Tate sat hunched at his table, where he did most of his writing. An empty beer bottle lay against the inkwell. Another bottle, half-full, stood at his elbow.

"Go on," he ordered.

Frank Warren resumed:

This arch-outlaw is now living amongst us in the best style which stolen money can buy, in the best rooms at the Rollins House in Cheyenne. His present alias is George Hansinger. To most of our citizens, Hansinger is outwardly a real estate operator. Only a few trusted lieutenants know his actual identity as chief of the Cheyenne bandits.

In the morning the indictment would be in the papers and ready for sale on the streets of Cheyenne. It would point out Hansinger, and necktie parties would surely be formed, to run him out of town if not to destroy him.

WARREN had assisted Tate in the long investigation, as they had painstakingly tracked down Hansinger, checking every bit of whispered information, every fact. They knew it was dangerous. During the job they had learned that George Hansinger was a ruthless killer. If one of his henchmen dared to cross him, it meant death.

"Let's make the type corrections," ordered Tate.

He rose, and helped Warren at the job. They ran off several final proof sheets and were spreading them on the table to dry when a voice spoke from the doorway.

"Good evening!"

The front door, like the windows, stood open. They had not heard the approach of the speaker, busy with their work as they had been, and with the sounds of Cheyenne in their ears. Tate turned, his bony shoulders hunched, to look at the man.

"Why—hello, Hansinger," he said. "What can I do for you?" Tate kept a cool head, standing with his back to the table on which the printed proofs lay, the ink on them shining in the lamplight.

Frank Warren froze where he stood. Hansinger! He had been thinking and writing about the man for days, and he knew Hansinger's awful power. On a wooden peg a few feet away hung a six-shooter in a leather holster, and Warren thought for a moment of lunging for it. But as his eyes moved, he caught the gleam of light on a double-barreled shotgun, held on the window sill, covering him.

Hastily he glanced at the other side of the room, and to the rear. He saw shadowy figures, and the terrifying black muzzles of guns. Behind Hansinger, at the front door, were several men.

Warren maintained a bold front, taking his cue from Tate, the editor. His eyes bored steadily into Hansinger, studying the man.

Hansinger was an elegant dresser—that was one of his foibles. He loved fine clothes. His dark broadcloth suit was perfectly fitted to his large, well-fleshed body. He wore a checked waistcoat, a pure-white stock filling the V at his throat, and a diamond stickpin scintillated in the yellow light. A soft hat was cocked on one side of his head, and his black boots were of the softest, best leather, so highly polished they could have been used as a mirror.

Plainly he was a vain man, and with reason, as far as his figure was concerned, but with his face it was different. At some time he had suffered an attack of smallpox and this had left his face scarred. To hide the pocks, Hansinger wore a neatly trimmed beard, crisp, and of a chestnut hue. It jerked up as his deep-set black eyes piercing and analytical, pinned the luckless editor.

"I've been watching you, Tate," he said in a low but clear voice. "You're not the only one who has spies around Cheyenne!"

"What are you talking about, Hansinger?" asked Tate.

He carried it off well, thought Frank Warren. But Hansinger was not to be sidetracked or fooled. He knew too much.

"There's no use in lying, Tate," he said flatly. "I heard you'd be around asking questions, and so I planted a couple of my boys in your way. Where's the information you've collected about me?"

Tate shrugged. He stood defensively, hands behind him on the table. It was about eleven P. M., and a few shots in the town would draw little attention—as both newspapermen knew, as they knew Hansinger's caliber.

Hansinger stepped across the room, evenly. Immediately his aides filled the doorway. One of them was a broad, red-headed fellow known as "Brick" Lowndes; another was the supple, dark-skinned gambler, Aloysius. They carried six-shooters in sight, but if Hansinger were armed, his weapons were concealed.

13

Guns covered Tate and Warren from every angle.

Hansinger reached the table, picked up one of the sheets, and began to read it. His beard jerked up and down as he silently mouthed the words, and Warren saw a brick-red color mounting over the growth on Hansinger's face. His high cheek-bones grew scarlet with rage as he perused the exposé, and his nostrils flared.

Hansinger crumpled the paper up, threw it on the floor. Without further warning, he whipped a short-barreled derringer from inside his coat and fired point-blank into the editor's heart.

Frank Warren saw only a blur as Hansinger drew the pistol to shoot, for Hansinger was most expert, no doubt from long and constant practise. Warren knew that his friend and mentor Tate was dead, before the editor thudded to the creaky wooden floor.

Warren reacted with the desperate speed of self-preservation. With a hoarse cry he threw himself to the floor, rolling closer to the heavy bulk of the printing press. A shotgun roared, and one of the oil lamps was hit by spreading buck.

A pellet cut the flesh of Warren's left arm, stung him frightfully, and brought a shrill cry from him. He seized a heavy form, filled with lead block letters and hurled it at the scowling Hansinger who had turned to deal with him. The man's deep-set eyes burned, his nostrils flared, his crisp beard pointed straight at Warren. The form hit Hansinger a glancing blow in the ribs and spoiled his aim.

Then Warren was behind the press. One wall of the office was blank, and for a moment he was sheltered. He began yelling for help at the top of his voice. If only it was dark in the room, he thought, in agony.

He clutched at a wrench which was used to tighten certain nuts on the press. The big lamp in the middle made him a fair target, and he flung the wrench at the light. The chimney crashed with a violent tinkle, and there was suddenly a brilliant flare as the chain on one side parted and tipped oil into the remnant of flame on the wick. The burning oil dropped in a sheet to the dry floor, and smoke rose.

"Let her burn!"

That was Hansinger, as his men seeing the fire start, sprang forward to put it out.

"Catch the young fool and slit his throat so he can't talk!" ordered Hansinger. "Move! We'll leave 'im here and let her burn. Best way."

A gunman let go with a blast of a shotgun, and the buck spattered the wall and the press near the crouched, hidden Warren.

"The trap-door!" he thought.

Close at hand was a two-foot-square opening which led under the flooring. It had been necessary to brace the underpinnings in order to support the weight of the press, and the hole served also as a storage place for odds and ends of junk.

Warren had been down it often enough, after something such as a piece of wire or a tool, or to clean the place out. He threw himself along the floor and seized the leather strap which acted as a handle to lift the trap-door. One end came off, so violently did he jerk at it, but the other held and the door came up.

He dived for it. A bullet from a Colt missed, and his legs squirmed out of sight.

The earth, with light coming through the lattice-work around the base of the building, was warm. Insects were thick here, but he did not heed the spider webs as he crawled hastily for the rear. He could hear the men overhead, the heavy treads, the voices. They had to catch him, for he was too dangerous a witness to let escape.

Warren had to crawl all the way, for the space was too shallow for him to stand in it. His knee hit a sharp stone, hurt frightfully, and his arm wound was bleeding, but in the desperate excitement he did not notice such things. His breath came in gasps. It seemed to take long minutes to reach the rear lattice, but he made it, kicked one corner of the section out with his foot, and crawled out.

In the narrow way behind the buildings Warren glimpsed horses not far away, standing with dropped reins. They belonged to Hansinger's men, who had rushed into the shop through doors and windows where the fight had begun. The young printer turned to run toward the mustangs, his first wild instinct being escape.

"There he goes!"

Aloysius had reached the back door of the office and had seen the darting figure as Warren sped toward safety. The tall gambler fired hastily, and Warren heard the lead, while the mustangs stamped and snorted uneasily at the flare of the big pistol. Then Brick Lowndes ran out and began to shoot.

Warren started to dodge like a rabbit as the lead whipped past him. He stumbled once and fell headlong, but picked himself up and darted on toward the frightened cayuses.

Now the cavvy was jerking at reins tied to clumps of brush. Several of the horses were already free, and they raced off in terror of the smash of powder and whine of lead. The gunmen trying to halt Warren apparently realized that one of their own broncs might get hit, for the shooting suddenly let up.

"Stop him!" Brick Lowndes shouted. "He's going to get a bronc."

The fugitive reached the cavvy.

Warren hit the nearest saddle without bothering with the stirrup. He had bent forward to pull the reins when something hit him. His head seemed to burst with a horrible roar, and he slumped in the leather seat.

CHAPTER II
Buffalo Bill

DUST swirled on the Wyoming plains. The earth trembled with the tons upon tons of buffaloes helplessly dying that men might eat. The heavy explosions of the Sharps rifles, each firing a ball which weighed eight to the pound, were monotonous in their deep-throated song of death.

The big animals lay dead on the dreary, sandy flat, covered with a low brush, where the skillful hunters had stalked them. The buffalo was stupid, too stupid to run away when one of his trail mates fell over. Great bulls, with shaggy, monstrous shoulders and massive heads topped by incurving horns, stared in bewilderment, awaiting each his turn. Smaller cows, and calves, nervously sniffing, slowly circled the herd.

"Seems a shame to kill 'em," muttered one of

18

the hunters, a man who was known from the Rio Grande to the Canadian borders as the Rio Kid.

The heavy rifle kicked against his trained shoulder, which took the recoil properly. Another buffalo slowly sank to his front knees and rolled over in the dust.

On the Rio Kid's right another heavy weapon roared—that was "Lucretia Borgia," as another of the hunters, a man who had become famous in the West as "Buffalo Bill" Cody had humorously dubbed his favorite rifle. Thousands of the animals had fallen before Lucretia Borgia, directed by the skillful ace of hunters, William F. Cody.

A third rifle sounded from the left. It belonged to a young Mexican, Celestino Mireles, trail-mate of the Rio Kid.

At last the kill was completed, and at Cody's signal the Rio Kid and Mireles ceased fire. The three sweated, dusty hunters stood up to stretch and, no longer concealed by the piles of brush they had fixed as stands from which to shoot, they were visible to the stupid survivors of the buffalo herd—runts, calves and some cows—which moved rapidly away, picking up speed.

The Rio Kid, whose real name was Bob Pryor, was a handsome young fellow, a trained hardened athlete. In the Union Army during the War, Pryor had been a captain of cavalry, riding under Custer and Sheridan. After the conflict his restless soul had sent him roving the dangerous frontier seeking the excitement he craved. He couldn't long abide the cramped ways of civilized communities.

In the Army Bob Pryor had been dashing and debonair, and he had clung to many things reminiscent of those exciting days, such as the blue shirt, the dark whipcord pants tucked into polished high boots he now wore, and the cavalryman's felt Stetson which covered his close-clipped chestnut hair. His face was tanned by sun and wind, and he exuded health; his chest was broad, his body tapered to the narrow waist of a true fighting man, and he was not too tall for an ideal cavalryman. Noted on the frontier as a man to have on your side, intrepid and cool in any sort of a fight, the Rio Kid's commanding air impressed beholders at first glance, made them trust him.

Crossed cartridge belts supported his Colt revolvers, and usually he carried another brace hidden under his shirt. His skill and speed with guns was well-known. As a lad in Texas he had learned to shoot and it came naturally, while constant practise kept him trained to a hair.

Buffalo Bill Cody waved at Pryor, and the Rio Kid strolled over to join him. The lean figure of Celestino slouched toward them. Old Brigham, Cody's buckskin mustang, was hidden with Pryor's dun, Saber, and Mireles's piebald gelding, behind the little rise from which they had crept to their stands to make the buffalo kill.

"Nice work," complimented Cody. "Yuh don't miss often, do yuh, Rio Kid?"

"Lead costs money." Bob Pryor smiled. "But this work is like shootin' at barn doors, Bill. Those critters got no sense of self-preservation."

"True enough," agreed Cody. "But men got to eat. General Dodge has twenty-five thousand workers on that railroad, and they got to down three a day or else. Money in it for us, too, yuh savvy."

Cody was a gloriously handsome man, tall, straight as an arrow, with flowing golden hair and beard. He had been a pony express rider, a scout for the Army, a soldier and Indian fighter. He was clad now in supple buckskin garments, fringed at the seams, and a wide brimmed Stetson. Chief of hunters for the Union Pacific, in his early thirties, Buffalo Bill had earned the respect of every decent human being. He had a charm of manner which fascinated both men and women.

He squatted down, and took a drink from a canteen. Celestino ambled up, leaned on his Sharps, watching the Rio Kid and Buffalo Bill.

Mireles was young, bony, and tall. He had an ascetic face, with high cheek-bones, dark eyes, and hawk nose. In his native Mexican clothing of tight-fitting pants and steeple sombrero, he was a striking figure, a good match for the Rio Kid and Cody.

EVER since shortly after the Civil War he had been the constant companion of the Rio Kid, for it had been after Pryor's return to his own despoiled Texas home that he had been able to snatch Mireles from death at the hands of bandits who had killed the Mexican youth's parents and burned his ancestral home. So Celestino had chosen to follow his "General," as he always called the Rio Kid, on the wild danger trails of the frontier.

The Rio Kid and Mireles rolled cigarettes as they rested after the kill of the buffaloes. Over the scene hung acrid powder smoke and dust, the aura of death. Yet men must eat.

"We'll ride back and signal the wagons to come pick up the meat," said Buffalo Bill. "We want to get it in before dark."

The three horses, Old Brigham, and Saber, and the beautiful gelding which Mireles was riding—the Mexican was an expert judge of horseflesh and enjoyed trading and getting the better of the bargain—awaited them. Saber was of mouse hue but the black stripe down his spine proclaimed him to be of "the breed that never dies." A trained cavalry mount, he loved the Rio Kid, and the two were comrades of the wild trails. He was ill-tempered with strangers, but would behave when so ordered by the Rio Kid.

The three men mounted, and rode up a long incline from which they could signal their skinners, who were with the big freight wagons which would carry the carved meat back to Dodge's railroad camp. The Rio Kid breasted the top of the hill first, and paused to look out across the vast expanses of southern Wyoming.

"Trail herd comin'," he said, turning in his saddle to speak to Buffalo Bill and Celestino. Joining him, they stared at the great clouds of dust far off in the wide spaces to the southwest.

"They got a bunch of wagons with 'em," remarked Cody.

The Rio Kid unshipped a pair of field-glasses and adjusted them to his eyes.

"Women with the wagons, Bill," he commented. "The outriders look like Texans. Reckon it's a herd from the Lone Star State. And they've come to stay."

"Yeah, reckon so." Buffalo Bill nodded. "Been quite a few folks headed to settle in Wyoming. Grass here is the best in the world."

The sun was bright, still yellow but moving toward the setting. The men pulled their reins, and rode north to pick up their skinners and vehicles they had left when it had become necessary to stalk the big herd they had slaughtered.

A mile away, they saw the flat wagons and figures of lounging men, waiting for them, and Cody signaled. The skinners and wagonmen came to life, and started driving toward them.

Buffalo Bill rode back toward the spot where the buffalo lay. Already there were specks in the sky, as the vultures eyed the dead carcasses, and there were plenty of other scavengers which would quickly ruin the meat. The wagonmen, watching Cody's figure, turned east, and disappeared in a draw between two small ridgelike hills.

The Rio Kid and Mireles leisurely followed.

"See, General!" exclaimed Celestino, pointing toward the lower ridge. "Ees Indian, *sí?*"

As a matter of course, they made ready for trouble.

Wyoming was a bone of contention between the mighty Sioux and Cheyenne Indians and the white invaders.

"He's alone!" exclaimed the Rio Kid. "He's tryin' to hide in them rocks. Looks like the wagons must have flushed him out of that draw!"

Curious, the Rio Kid turned toward the spot. He had cleaned and cased the heavy Sharps hunting rifle which now rode in a special boot by his leg. He picked up his light carbine and checked it, throwing a shell into the breech, holding it across the pommel ready for action.

' The wagons, coming fast and raising high dust, came into view as the riders emerged from the draw. The drivers obeyed the pointing rifle of Buffalo Bill who was heading for the kill. The Rio Kid kept on toward the dark spot where he could see the Indian among the rocks, trying to hide, but there was not sufficient cover.

"See if we can scare him out," he said to

Celestino, and put a carbine slug within a foot of the skulking savage.

It brought results. A piece of whitish rag was waved violently above the rock. Closer in, alert and with his carbine, aimed, the Rio Kid caught the red man's cries on the wind:

"No shoot—me friend! No shoot!"

Near the foot of the sharply rising ridge, the Rio Kid drew up Saber. "Come out of there with yore hands up, whoever yuh are!" he sang out.

CHAPTER III
Friendly Indian

STILL waving the flag of truce, the Indian emerged and came hesitantly toward the two riders. A couple of mustangs galloped around the ridge, sparking away into the distance. They carried no riders. It looked as though the wagons had flushed them from the draw.

The Rio Kid and Mireles gazed with curiosity on the bizarre figure of the Indian as he came up to them, his hands high. The red man was afraid they meant to kill him but dared not disobey. He was a well-formed Indian, and tall, but the clothing he wore was in tatters, and did not suit the savage's frame. It had been made from remnants of an old horse blanket. He wore a ridiculous little hat, the brim of a beaver head-dress which had at some long time past belonged to a wealthy white. Braids hung to his shoulders under this.

"You Crow?" inquired the Rio Kid.

The man nodded violently. "Me Crow. White man's friend. No do nothin'. Good boy. Johnny Three Snakes, me."

"Yuh got a gun hid under your shirt," the Rio Kid accused.

"Me find, no stealum. Me white man's friend." Johnny Three Snakes had a desperate, hunted look in his black eyes.

"What'd yuh run away for when the wagons come—" began Pryor, but broke off. On the wind he had caught an unearthly, wailing cry. It came from over the crest of the ridge, near where they had first seen the Crow.

"Yuh got somebody up there!" he shouted. "Take his hardware, Celestino. Watch him, now!"

The Mexican threw himself to the ground, and leaped behind Johnny Three Snakes. He removed a six-shooter from inside the Indian's shirt, and confiscated a hunting knife.

"Has mon-ees, too," Celestino said. "Seex dollaires—a watch. Look like he rob white hombre!"

"No stealum—me friend!" wailed the Crow.

But under the stern gun muzzle he miserably trudged up the hill, and the Rio Kid, with his Mexican *compadre*, followed afoot, since the slope was too much for a horse. At the crest, they slid over a bank, into the cut. Pausing, the Rio Kid could see a blanket-swathed figure hidden by bulging rock strata from the center

27

of the depression, which route Cody's wagons had followed as they went through.

There was a little camp here, bivouac. In it was a prostrate man, a couple of canteens, a jackrabbit's skeleton, freshly flensed of meat. There were flies and other insects over the skin of the rabbit, over the chunks of soft pinkish meat, and on the helpless white man lying there partly wrapped in a blanket.

The Rio Kid, kneeling beside the injured, delirious fellow, could make out a few of his tortured words. He would break off now and then to wail:

"Help me! Stop—please—stop!"

"No hurtum," growled Johnny Three Snakes.

"You shot him?" demanded the Rio Kid.

"No shootum." The Crow was sullen now. Plainly he had expected to be blamed. "Shootum in Cheyenne."

"Who did shoot him then?"

Johnny Three Snakes shrugged. He regretted now the altruistic impulse which had caused him to spring from the darkness, grab a horse and ride out of town with Frank Warren who was slumped unconscious on another horse beside him. Johnny could speak some English, and understood more, but it was difficult, almost impossible, to explain in detail to the Rio Kid. How could he tell this strange white man that Warren had given him money and food, had been his friend? In Johnny Three Snakes was a never-ending struggle between the savage impulses of his inborn nature, and the veneer he had acquired by associating with the strange whites. At one time he had attended a mission school and he had worked on white men's ranches. But he still went along with other Crow braves, to kill the Sioux and Cheyenne enemies. At such times he went naked save for a breech-cloth, and was painted like any other savage. And he would steal any horse that he believed he could get away with.

He had made an earnest effort to understand the mental processes of the race which was obviously the more powerful—and the Crows had been the white man's allies from the start, chiefly because the Crows hated the Sioux and Cheyennes for harassing and attacking them throughout their history. But the complicated thought of the white man was too much for Johnny Three Snakes.

FOR INSTANCE, if a man killed another, then he must be killed. That was sensible. But instead of letting the most wronged do it—the nearest blood relative—the white man insisted on locking the culprit in a little house with bars on the window, making a big fuss, talking, always talking, until finally they would hang the man. It came to the same thing in the end, but the white man wasted so much time and effort.

And horses! Johnny Three Snakes' father had gone to the greatest of pains to teach his little son how to be an expert horse thief. It was a game, a great occupation, among the Crows. A brave who could steal a good horse from another person, without the latter even suspecting what was going on, was given a feast and congratulated. But the white man— he would hang you for it.

Johnny Three Snakes, confused by so many contradictions between the philosophies of the two races, was like a child who is learning what is right and wrong in the world. The child cannot say whether or not what it does is good or bad until it is praised or punished.

The Rio Kid had made a quick examination of the tall slender young fellow who lay in the blanket. Dark smudges showed on his tortured, pain-wracked face, and his clothing was dirty and torn. He wore an old blue shirt and a pair of overalls, and one shoe was missing. The brown eyes were heavily underlined, wide and staring but anguished in spite of their vacuous expression.

Pryor found a small wound in the upper part of the man's left arm. But the chief injury was beneath the curly dark hair which was matted with dried blood and bits of scalp. Carefully the Rio Kid investigated this. It was a deep furrow and he thought that the bullet still remained under the swollen bulge where it had buried itself after creasing the skull.

"Who shot him?" he growled again, standing up and scowling threateningly at Johnny Three Snakes.

"Bad man shootum," the Indian said sullenly.
"Me no shootum. He Three Snakes' friend."

"What's his handle—his name?"

Johnny Three Snakes thought it over.
"Frank."

"He's from Cheyenne?"

The Crow only shrugged.

"Here ees wallet, General," Celestino said.
"Ees leetle card. Say 'Frank Warren. Cheyenne
Times.'"

Pryor studied the smudged card which
Mireles had extracted.

"Reckon this feller is Frank Warren, then,"
he said. "He must work for the paper in Cheyenne. He needs attention right off, too. That
slug's pressin' his brain-pan. We'll take the
Crow back to Cheyenne, too, and see if we can
find out what's what."

It was a mystery he had chanced upon, and
he meant to assist Warren, who was suffering,
and out of his head from the skull wound.

Johnny Three Snakes grew as excited as an
Indian could.

"No take Cheyenne! Killum dere!"

"Who will?" growled the Rio Kid.

"Bad men. Shootum! I fetch here. My friend.
Giveum Johnny mon-ee. No take Cheyenne."

The Rio Kid was beginning to like Johnny
Three Snakes. The Crow was desperately trying to explain, though he was not sure of his
position. He was thinking that perhaps he had
broken another white man's rule by snatching

Warren from death. That had happened some years before, when two of Johnny's friends had been put in jail for helping out a white acquaintance who turned out to be an outlaw.

Pryor looked over the little camp. It was plain that someone, undoubtedly the Crow, had been feeding rabbit blood to the injured man, to give him strength. If the Indian had wished to kill Warren he could easily have done so with his knife or gun as the white man lay helpless.

The Rio Kid changed his opinion of the Indian. Perhaps it was as Three Snakes claimed, that Warren was his friend and that, after the newspaperman had been hurt by enemies in Cheyenne, the Crow had saved him from death.

The sun was reddening. Dark would fall inside of another hour. Cheyenne was the nearest settlement, and it was some twenty miles northwest. But the Crow said that Warren would be killed there.

The Rio Kid hesitated. He might run Warren up to Dodge's railroad camp, which at the moment lay northeast of the draw, but the jogging would not help the wounded man. Warren was gasping for breath. He needed quick attention and rest.

AS HE squatted, thinking what he could do to save the young fellow's life, the low rumbling of the earth increased. The sound came from west of the draw, and the van of the steers, heading north, began slowly passing, heads lowered, tired from the day's run. Glimpses of swift riders, the shouts of the cowboys, told the Rio Kid that the trail drivers were making ready to turn the herd and bed down for the night.

He recalled that they had wagons along, and women.

"Best thing for him," he said musingly. "We'll tote him over and see what's what."

Before the Rio Kid could prepare the wounded man for travel and reach the trail drive and the wagons, the lumbering vehicles had turned off the trail cut by the thousands of cattle hoofs, and had been drawn up in a circle near a brook, a feeder of Lodgepole Creek. Men were watering the draught animals, while women in cotton dresses with wide, flowing skirts and sunbonnets were busy getting a fire started and food from the wagon boxes to prepare the evening meal. Up the line, tall young Texas men were quieting the steers, and seeing to them.

The approach of the Rio Kid and Mireles, with Frank Warren's body slung between them in a sling improvised from the horse blanket, and with Johnny Three Snakes trotting ahead, had not gone unnoticed. Keen eyes were always on the watch. This head had come all the way up from Texas, through Indian territory, and eternal vigilance had been the watchword. There were both red and white raiders in the land, and no law, no protection save what a man could furnish for himself.

Each man was ready for whatever might happen!

CHAPTER IV
Good Samaritans

CURIOUS eyes sought the Rio Kid and his companions as they pulled up at the edge of camp. The Rio Kid sang out and made the signs of friendship familiar to people of the plains. Dismounting then, he helped Mireles and the Crow lower Warren to the ground. Some of the cowboys, with the herd turned and brought to a halt, had come galloping back when they had seen the strangers approaching.

The men were big fellows for the most part, stalwart of body, and heavily armed. They wore leather and great Stetsons with curving brims, and their weather-reddened faces were proud and grim. The Rio Kid knew their kind, for he had been one of them. He could speak their language and understood how they felt. Texas had fought on the loser's side of the war and, uprooted by carpetbaggers or the devasta-

35

tion of the recent conflict, many Confederates had moved West or North, or even into Mexico and South America, hunting a new start.

A girl stood near by. She had pushed back her blue sunbonnet from her thick golden hair that was done in neat braids. Her long-lashed blue eyes were a striking feature in her beautiful, youthful face. Her red lips were parted as she stared at the lithe Rio Kid, then at the gasping, restless Warren, writhing in agony on the blanket where he lay.

She started forward.

"Oh, the poor fellow!" she cried. "What's wrong with him, sir?"

The Rio Kid touched his hat brim, saluting her. Any man would have been affected by her, and the Rio Kid was no exception.

"He's bad hurt, ma'am," he said. "Needs attention."

A tall young fellow with thick curly black hair and a fire-eater's eyes stepped out and confronted Pryor, who nodded and smiled.

"I'm the Rio Kid," he introduced himself. "I got a wounded hombre here, mister."

The self-appointed delegate scowled. "Never heard of yuh," he replied coldly. "Is that moth-eaten Injun part of yore gang? Keep him off. He don't look good, and we don't cotton to redskins."

The Rio Kid's temper rose in a flare of angry resentment. But Bob Pryor was a man of experience, and he had command of himself. He

36

bit off the sharp retort on the end of his tongue, coolly appraising the young Texan. As the fellow remained silent, an older man came forward, his hand outstretched.

"I'll palaver with him, Drew," he said, and there was a hint of admonishment in his voice.

The girl with the fair hair had moved toward the wounded Warren, and stooped to look more closely at him.

"Suh," the older man said to the Rio Kid, "I am Gus Jennings, and these are my friends and relatives, all from the Brazos country of Texas. We're on our way to settle in Wyomin'. Yore handle sounds like yuh might be a Texan yore ownself."

"I am, Colonel—from the Rio Grande, though I ain't been home for quite a long while."

The Rio Kid shook Jennings' big, toil-calloused hand. The colonel was a stout man with a florid face, the flesh over his cheek-bones flecked by strawberry marks. He wore a mustache and a goatee, gray-tinged like his light hair, though the difference in shades was hard to detect at a distance. His sturdy frame was clad in leather trousers, a butternut shirt, a Confederate cavalryman's Stetson, and cavalry boots covered his stocky legs. He did not need to say he had been an officer in one of the Southern armies.

Others came crowding around, curious to see what it was all about, but the Rio Kid quickly realized that Gus Jennings was the leader. The dark young fire-eater had exceeded his authority in challenging the Rio Kid.

"I got a young hombre here by the handle of Frank Warren—reckon he's a printer or newspaper feller," explained the Rio Kid. "Just found him, lyin' wounded over in that draw, Colonel. This here Crow Injun was takin' care of him and I believe he saved Warren's life. Warren's got a nasty head wound, and some other injuries not as serious. What he needs is a rest and some attention. Can yuh help out?"

"Most assuredly, suh," Jennings said promptly, and called to a plump, sweet-faced woman of middle age, who had been busy at one of the big canvas-topped wagons: "Oh, Mother!"

He introduced the Rio Kid to his wife, and Sara Jennings went with them toward where young Warren lay.

"I see my little girl's already tryin' to help," said Jennings, smiling. "This is my daughter Alyse, suh . . . Alyse, I would like to present the Rio Kid, from Texas originally."

SHE HAD a quick smile for the debonair Rio Kid as she looked up at him.

"Mother," she announced, "there's a slug under this poor man's scalp. I believe it's what's hurting him so."

"He's out of his head," said the Rio Kid. "Reckon that bullet's pressin' in on his skull."

Frontier women and their men were accus-

tomed to dealing with physical injuries, with
gunshot wounds and cuts, and many developed
real skill in treating such hurts. And Colonel
Jennings, because of his experience in the war,
knew more than most people about bullet
wounds.

"Needs to come out, but it'll have to be
done careful or else we'll permanently injure
the brain," he said, after a close examination
of Warren. "Oh, Bert! You, Drew—Tim—over
here."

Jennings himself took the fourth corner of
the blanket litter. He wished to move Warren
without undue pain for the young fellow. They
carried him to a wagon, where a blanket bed
was made, and he could have protection. Mrs.
Jennings filled a pan with clean water from
the brook, upstream from where the cattle had
roiled the feeder. Alyse Jennings sat beside the
wounded man, soothing him.

"Dinner'll be ready in a jiffy," said Colonel
Jennings hospitably. "It ain't much, suh, but
yuh'd do us an honor if yuh'd stay."

"Thanks amighty, Colonel," said the Rio Kid.
"We'll appreciate it."

Women were at the fire cooking strips of
dried beef and coffee. They had home-made
bread in a big box, baked at some previous
stopping place. Jennings introduced the Rio
Kid around. Two of the men in the colonel's
party held the title of major, a couple were
captains, some were lieutenants or sergeants—

all military ranks in the erstwhile Confederate forces.

These were the older men, the heads of the families, of which there were a dozen. They held proud names of old Texas—Taylor, McNeill, Lytle, Bishop, Daggett, Jackson. There was always a Jackson. Most of them had their wives and older daughters along, a number of smaller children, and the young fellows were their sons.

The Rio Kid knew at once that he would be leaving the injured Warren in the best of hands. When the water was hot, Mrs. Jennings and Alyse began cleaning Warren up and making him more comfortable. They had some beef and herb broth which they fed him by the spoonful.

Johnny Three Snakes, embarrassed by the crowd of whites, never said a word. He crouched near the edge of camp, watching the white men. Mireles kept an eye on him, while the Rio Kid made friends with the Texans.

Night was fast approaching, with the sun ready to dip behind the western horizon. They ate the hot meal, welcome to the Rio Kid and his Celestino, and to all the hard working men. A plate of food was taken over to Johnny Three Snakes.

But the Rio Kid had to decline the invitation to spend the night at the Texans' camp.

"Bill Cody'll be worried about me," he told Jennings, to whom he had explained the reason for his presence on the plains. "I'll have to get on back to the buffalo kill."

One of the cowboys had driven in the two horses which Johnny Three Snakes had used when he had brought Frank Warren out of Cheyenne. The Rio Kid turned them over to the Crow.

"Yuh can ride with me if yuh want to, Johnny," he said, "or yuh can go on about yore business, savvy?"

The Crow grunted. His broad face showed as much relief as he could express.

"Me go."

He leaped on one of the mustangs, kicked its ribs with his heels. Leading the other mustang, he tore away, low over his mount. Once he glanced back, just to make sure no one meant to shoot him. He disappeared over the rise at full-tilt.

Dark fell, and the stars and a swollen, distorted moon were furnishing what light there was when the Rio Kid and Mireles mounted and said so long to the Texans.

"I'll find yuh and see how Warren's doin', before too long, colonel," said Pryor, as he shook hands. "Thanks amighty for everything."

"It was a pleasure, suh," the colonel said heartily.

The Rio Kid and Celestino rode east and then north, headed for the position of the buffalo kill. Before many miles they picked up the red glow of Cody's fire and hurried to it.

Buffalo Bill came out to greet the Rio Kid, in reply to Pryor's shouts. It was always safer to announce one's approach to friends in the wilds.

"Where in tarnation blazes yuh been, Rio Kid?" cried Cody. "I was growin' worried about yuh."

"Tell yuh all about it."

THE Rio Kid dismounted, and saw to the dun, unsaddling Saber for the night, rubbing him down. He rolled a smoke then, and over a bottle shared with Buffalo Bill, informed Cody of all that had occurred.

"Those folks are right about Wyomin'," Cody remarked, nodding. "It's the best range I ever saw, Rio Kid. The grasses are the richest in the land and yuh never have to worry over water."

The skinners had been busy in the daylight hours. Now millions of flies and other insects buzzed over the hides and flesh, over the bones of the dead buffalo. Joints and tongues had been loaded into the wagons, and tarpaulins thrown over the meat.

In the near distance, the mournful howls of coyotes filled the air, and now and then they glimpsed a pair of glowing eyes, as the "buffalo wolves" impatiently waited for the men to clear out so they could eat what was left.

The Rio Kid and his friends slept on the spot, although a guard was maintained throughout the night to drive off the raiding animals and watch for chance Indian attack.

In the morning, they had coffee, meat, and hard bread. The skinners and wagonmen had the vehicles loaded down with meat, and would soon start for the railroad camp. The Rio Kid, Mireles and Buffalo Bill planned to hunt again during the day, and other wagons would come up with them.

They saw the wagons off and, saddling up, started to look for a good herd of buffalo on which to work. Around noon, they sighted the empty wagons coming toward them, and rode forward to signal them.

One of the drivers stood up, waving his hat over his head. He wanted to speak to them.

"Go see what he wants," said Cody. "I'll keep an eye on the buffalo."

The Rio Kid galloped across the half-mile of intervening plain. A tobacco-chewing wagon driver held out an envelope.

"General Dodge told me to give yuh this, Rio Kid," he said.

The Rio Kid opened the note. It was an order from General Grenville Dodge, Chief Engineer of the Union Pacific and read:

Please report to me as soon as possible. I have an important mission for you. Tell Cody I am sending another hunter to take your place.

Dodge

Nodding, the Rio Kid thrust the note in his pocket, with a regretful glance toward where Buffalo Bill waited.

CHAPTER V
Dangerous Assignment

NIGHT was close at hand when the Rio Kid rode up to General Dodge's temporary headquarters at railhead. It was a freight car fitted with a desk, chairs, and a couple of bunks.

The gangs were working, laying track, east of Cheyenne, and Dodge as a rule had to be here, there and everywhere, because of myriad duties that were his. He could seldom remain long in one spot. The task he had undertaken was an all but super-human one, and few could have carried it through as Dodge was doing, with his tremendous mental and physical energy.

Under the General's expert supervision, work began at the first touch of the dawn and was carried on without a break until the final light of day faded away. His surveyors had to move fast to keep up with the builders of the new transcontinental line.

'From his long military experience, Dodge had organized his twenty-five thousand men into an army, with each man knowing his exact duty. So many men dumped ties, another bunch leveled, others handled ties with spiked sticks; so many laid rails, while more drove the spikes. He had picked hardened young men, soldiers from the late conflict, for the most part, and they could maintain the pace he demanded.

They were at it now, racing as usual. The Rio Kid, pausing to roll a smoke after his quick ride in from the plains, shook his head in wonderment at the sight. It always amazed him, the way Dodge could get work out of his men.

A light car drawn by a strong horse dashed to the front with a load of rails. Two men grasped the near end, and others took hold as it was pulled off the car, all moving at a dog-trot.

"Let her go!" a man bawled.

The rail was let fall into position, and on the other side of the car a second gang had already dragged out the matching rail. At such a rate those men could lay four rails a minute. And when the car was emptied, it was tipped over on its side to let the next loaded one through.

But getting men to work without loss of time was only one of Dodge's triumphs. Constant Indian raids went on against the whites who were cutting the savage empire in twain and invading the red man's domain, and they had to be put down. Dodge also had organized his supply, so that his workers would never be short of the necessary materials.

In the dimming light, the Rio Kid saw a dominant figure, a man working harder than any of the others. It was General Grenville Dodge himself, giving a hand with the manual labor. Dodge would have built the railroad single-handed if he had been forced to, thought Pryor.

The darkness came quickly. Work was knocked off, and the weary laborers and drivers and foremen went to the tent camp to eat, to carouse a bit, perhaps, before sleeping until the first show of dawn.

"Evenin', General," said the Rio Kid, as Dodge turned away and came toward him.

"Rio Kid!" greeted the General. "I expected you. Been waiting for you. Come inside."

Grenville Dodge led the way into the freight car, into which small windows had been cut. He struck a match and lighted an oil lantern hanging from a strut across the middle of the car.

"Sit down, sit down," he invited heartily. "Have a drink."

Dodge was a masterful character and a striking figure of a man. He had a handsome head, with thick curly hair, and he sported a walrus mustache. His nose was large, his quick eyes

46

set deep. He was wearing a pair of old blue Army trousers and a wool Army shirt, open at the throat, and engineer's boots.

The Rio Kid thought a great deal of Dodge, and admired him tremendously, especially admiring such accomplishments in so young a man. Not yet forty, Dodge had been a pioneer railroad builder from the time he had graduated from Norwich University in Vermont. A son of poor parents, he had made his own way. Abraham Lincoln had met Dodge, had conferred with him before the great emancipator had been elected President—and Lincoln had never forgotten Dodge.

Dodge had been swept into the Civil War, had fought for the Union, been a high officer of engineers. Close to the end of the conflict, Lincoln had ordered Dodge from the Army and had made him a major-general, putting him in charge of the Union Pacific construction.

Now Lincoln, whom the Rio Kid, too, had known and loved, was dead, killed by a mad assassin.

Dodge took a box, which served as a seat, across the table from the Rio Kid. He picked up a stale sandwich made of a strip of meat and hard bread and began to munch his supper, drinking now and then, as he talked. He had to use every second in the twenty-four hours.

He came directly to the point.

"I sent for you, Rio Kid," he said, "because a serious problem has developed. We're nearing Cheyenne, which will be an important stop for the road. A number of my boys, who have run into the settlement during their time off, have been knocked over the head, robbed, and beaten. Several have been killed when they resisted. Last night I lost Hank Jansen, one of my best foremen, and a young engineer named Roberts, with the surveying parties up ahead, was killed last week in the center of Cheyenne.

"It's been reported to me that there's an organization in the town responsible for all this dirty work. They are lot-jumpin', too, trying to hold up the railroad, and seize the best locations. I know that you've done a good deal of investigative work—President Lincoln thought highly of you, and Custer and Sheridan both have spoken of you to me. I want you to go quietly into Cheyenne, look things over, and see how we can smash this outlaw bunch which has taken over.

"You might compare this to espionage work. You're a soldier and know how important that is. I'll give you all the support I can."

"Yes, sir." The job was right up the Rio Kid's alley, and though he was sorry to leave Buffalo Bill Cody, in a way he was glad to escape from the wholesale slaughter of the stupid buffalo. "If it's all right, General, I'd like to take my pard, Celestino Mireles, with me."

48

"Very well. He's with Cody now, isn't he?"
Dodge had a wonderful memory for details.

"That's right."

"I'll send two hunters out to take your places
with Cody. They can tell Mireles to join you in
Cheyenne. Good luck. You can find me when
you want me."

Dodge held out his hand. There were several
men outside the car, impatiently waiting to
speak to him.

The Rio Kid took his leave of the chief engineer. The new assignment pleased him, and
there was a smile on his face. It offered a welcome change and the fact that it might prove
decidedly dangerous only made it more stimu-
lating to the Rio Kid.

Leaving the railhead, he wasted no time,
but headed immediately for the wild Wyoming
settlement. . . .

Cheyenne stood on a broad plain, where the
gradual slope of the prairies met the steepening
grades of the Laramie mountains. Its altitude
was six thousand feet and the air was bracing,
cool. Because Dodge had decided to build extensive railroad shops at the spot, it had
assumed added importance, becoming a real
town overnight.

The Rio Kid, standing on the veranda of
the largest saloon, gazed upon the teeming
scene before him. It had not taken him long
to reach Cheyenne after seeing Dodge.

It was nearing midnight, the witching hour

for drinkers, their dance hall girl friends, and thieves. Raucous howls rose over Cheyenne which was made up of rough shacks galore, and tents set everywhere without regard to street alignment. Frames of new buildings stood waiting for the workmen to arrive in the morning. There was a saloon every square yard, it seemed—saloons in tents, and saloons in more elaborate quarters.

Hurdy-gurdies, grinding out tinny music for celebrants, conflicted with horrible discord. Camp-fires flickered along the banks of Crow Creek, and there also loomed the dim shapes of big canvas-topped wagons, heralding new arrivals in Wyoming; either to settle near Cheyenne, or to go on westward. Some planned to enter the Black Hills by this route, the easiest way into the forbidden mountains where lived the Sioux Indians, but where gold had been discovered.

The spaces and alleyways between the tents and shacks swarmed with every type of mankind—trappers, hunters, laborers, trainmen, engineers, lawyers, artists, gamblers, soldiers, promoters, gunmen. Indians of various tribes, too, were here. Sioux, Cheyennes, Pawnees, and others were roaming about, staring at the strange sights.

Water wells had been dug at the four corners of what was intended to be a business block, and in some places men with shotguns watched night and day to keep off lot-jumpers who were always watching a chance to seize some favorable location. Thieves as well as the sporting elements were enjoying a field day. Every man wore a gun, but usually only for his own personal protection. There was little civic organization to combat the undesirables who had swarmed in and taken over.

Merchants, enterprising men quick to seize a chance to make large profits, had opened up in tents or shacks. "Fashion Bazaar," proclaimed a painted sign over a big canvas-walled place. "California Meat Market," said another.

INTO this welter of over-stimulated, hypersensitive humanity the Rio Kid meant to plunge in his attempt to ferret out the outlaw bunch which General Dodge believed had assumed control in Cheyenne.

Bob Pryor was content merely to observe the town during the remainder of the evening, so he moved from spot to spot, watching the gamblers and the sport which went on. There had been a fire, a recent one, for the blackened embers of a wooden building had gone up in smoke and with it half a block of tents and nondescript shacks had been burned before the bucket brigades, abetted by a street break, had managed to get it under control. The Rio Kid asked a townsman what the fire had destroyed.

"That was the newspaper, mister—Cheyenne *Times*, she was," he was informed. "Went up in smoke last Monday, just before the weekly edition was due. The editor got burnt up in the fire."

The Rio Kid stood looking at the mess, the black ruins of what had been the *Times*. He remembered the young fellow he had found in Johnny Three Snakes' company—what was his name, now—Warren, that was it. Warren had worked for the Cheyenne *Times*.

The old fellow he had questioned was willing enough to talk, to show his knowledge to the stranger.

"What was this editor hombre's handle?" asked the Rio Kid.

"Tate. Paul Tate. Good feller, too, and a fine editor."

"I see. Somebody told me the editor of yore sheet was named Warren."

"Oh, that was Frank, young Frank," said the informant. "He was Tate's helper. They ain't found his body let. Figger it was all burnt up in the blaze. She shore got hot."

"Quite a town you got here," the Rio Kid observed. "Looks excitin'. I thought I might hang around a while if I could find somethin' interestin'."

"Yuh can find anything yuh're a-mind to in Cheyenne, stranger," boasted the citizen.

"My line is cattle. I come from Texas."

A couple of men, one rather tall and with a cadaverous face, glided past. They wore six-shooters and dark clothing—were sober, too—and they slowed, to eye the men talking on the corner. The Rio Kid, who was trained to a hair in such matters from long experience on the frontier and through the war, when such decisions meant life or death, felt a rising of the hackles. An old wound in his side began to itch, a sure warning of danger.

The two men eyed him speculatively. But he did not look to be an easy victim, and the oldster wore poor clothing. The pair passed on to the next turn and went around the block.

"Wild bunch in town, I hear," prodded the Rio Kid.

The elderly citizen glanced quickly into his eyes, looked away, and shrugged. "I reckon I better get on home to bed," he said. "I work tomorrer mornin'. S'long, stranger. Watch yore hair."

He hurried off in the direction opposite to that taken by the two armed, silent fellows.

The Rio Kid strolled on. He paused at the lamplighted corner to peer down the dark side street, but the two armed gentry were no longer in sight. He went on, passing the offices of the Cheyenne & Black Hills Stage Line. The painted sign outside announced:

SHORTEST. SAFEST. BEST.

SIX-HORSE CONCORD STAGES DAILY

FOR POINTS IN THE BLACK HILLS

The Government had deeded the Hills to the Sioux in perpetuity, but men of adventurous mold knew that gold was there, and Cheyenne the nearest town to the hills.

The settlement howled in the night.

"Reckon I'll go pick up Saber and my bedroll and turn in for a snooze," thought the Rio Kid, yawning.

As he was headed for the Bon Ton Corral, where he had left his horse, he caught the sharp crack of pistol shots from the north end of the town. They drew him back. But by the time he got there the usual crowd had collected, staring at a dead man who had two bullet-holes in him, one through the back of the head. His pockets had been turned inside out, obviously rifled.

A town marshal with a five-pointed silver star was turning the victim over. He found a card which read:

JOHN Y. FREDERIKS
Civil Engineer

"Looks like another railroad worker, gents," said the marshal in a slow voice.

54

CHAPTER VI
Wild Town

BOB PRYOR, the Rio Kid, pushed through the crowd and got a good look at the dead face. He thought he recognized Frederiks as a technician he had seen around Dodge's headquarters. So this was the sort of thing Dodge had sent him to check!

"I seen him over at the Elite, Marshal!" a loafer piped up. "He won three thousand at the roulette wheel, and he was mighty tickled with hisself."

"Reckon somebody else seen him, too, and is now mighty tickled with *hisself!*" a wag said dryly.

The crowd laughed and the tension broke. The marshal and a couple of friends were removing the body. There were no witnesses to the crime—at least no one would admit having seen anybody running from the scene.

The Rio Kid looked around for a few minutes but he realized that the killers would have left the spot as soon as they had disposed of their victim. He started away, but the excitement had made him thirsty, and the Elite was across the dirt street. It was a large saloon, wide-open, and with a dance hall, bar, and gambling devices of every sort.

But closer at hand was the Rollins House bar, the best place in town. The Rio Kid decided on it, went in and pushed his way to the long bar. The barkeepers were busy serving customers and he had to wait. But when his drink had been served and he was lifting it, he saw a couple of customers enter by a side way. He watched them in the big mirror behind the bar, and recognized the tall one as the cadaverous-faced fellow who had given him the eye when he had been talking to the oldster on the street. He believed the other had been the tall man's companion.

They interested him now because they were out of breath. They had been running.

"Could they have done that killin'?" he asked himself.

Intrigued, the Rio Kid observed them, always in the mirror, so he did not have to turn around. They acted as men might who have completed a task. They were thirsty and called for whisky, tossing down three glasses before they were satisfied. Then the tall one moved to a table where a game of stud poker was going on and bought into the game. His comrade favored the roulette wheel.

"Guess I won't turn in—yet," decided the Rio Kid.

He had another drink, and went to the edge of the dance floor, waiting until he could get a chair, from which spot he could watch the two fellows gambling without appearing to.

It was a boresome wait. The clock over the bar read 2:35 before the tall, bony-faced man quit, having lost a large roll. He yawned, went over for a nightcap, then to consult with his friend, who was still at the wheel. The stocky man nodded and passed some money to the cadaverous-faced one, who left the saloon.

The Rio Kid watched him duck under the hitch-rail to which horses could be tied and which prevented the animals from getting onto the wooden sidewalk. The fellow went across the street, and toward a side door opening from the big Elite into the street which ran into the main one close at hand. The Rio Kid took a chance and picked up speed. He glimpsed the lean figure turning left down a hallway just inside the open entry of the Elite.

He was putting in a lot of time on shreds of circumstantial evidence, mused the Rio Kid. But he had to start somewhere and the hunch he now had was too strong to ignore. Perhaps the bony-faced gambler lived in the Elite, but the Rio Kid meant to investigate anyhow. Then he was inside the place, and could see the main saloon through a wide opening to the right. The man he was trailing went into a room opening off the hall.

That curiosity was not advisable in Cheyenne, the Rio Kid was well aware. If his idea was right, that the tall gambler had robbed Frederiks, it would be fatal to be caught snooping. He went down the hall, trying to avoid loose, creaking boards, and paused, leaning against the wall just before he came to the private room. The door stood ajar and he could hear a buzz of voices.

"I hear yuh done all right tonight, Mac," he heard a man's voice say. "Marshal Wygant says yuh got over three thousand dollars."

"Yeah, Brick. My pardner Jim and me. Easy come, easy go, though. I just lost my shirt in that stud game over across the street." Mac, the cadaverous-faced man, guffawed, but there was no answering mirth.

"Ha-ha," the man called Brick said dryly. "I hope yuh didn't lose it *all*, Mac."

"Can't yuh take a joke, Brick? I held out yore cut, and Jimmy sent his by me. There yuh are. One hundred, two hundred, three hundred." Mac counted out a thousand dollars.

"All right," said Brick. "Keep the pennies. We're fair enough if yuh play square with us, Mac."

58

"Oh, we'll do that, Brick. Well, reckon I'll turn in."

IT WAS time to move, and the Rio Kid started walking just as the bony Mac hurried from the room, and bumped into him.

"Oh—sorry, mister," said Mac.

"No offense—my fault, mister," replied the Rio Kid softly.

He nodded, and Mac went toward the front, while he kept on down the hall as though he belonged there and had simply been passing when Mac barged out. As he went by the door he could see the lighted gambling room with a round table at which sat five men, glasses and chips and cards before them. They had been immersed in the game when Mac had arrived.

One had a shock of startlingly red hair over a wide, freckled face. His nose was squashed against his ugly skull, and he was broad of body. In the glimpse he had, the Rio Kid noted the fierce, greenish eyes which glanced up at him.

"That'll be Brick," he decided, and then he was past the opening.

He went out a rear door, passed the Elite's stables and corral, and made his way to the main thoroughfare in time to see Mac and his partner Jim mounting horses. They did not ride far, though—only up the way to a small shack which they entered, evidently to sleep.

It was after three when the Rio Kid finally turned in, near the corral where he had left Saber.

"Looked like Mac and his pard paid a cut to Brick on that hold-up job," he mused, as he sought sleep.

He meant to keep his eye on Mac and Jim, and on Brick. . . .

Celestino Mireles rode up the main street of Cheyenne late the next morning, and the Rio Kid, who was up and had breakfast, signaled him. They retired behind a convenient building, where they could talk without being observed by the whole settlement. True to his promise, Dodge had sent a hunter to take the Mexican's place with Buffalo Bill, and had ordered Mireles to join the Rio Kid.

Pryor quickly told his friend what he had already discovered.

"This Brick hombre has a couple rooms at the Elite, I find," he informed Celestino. "S'pose you sashay over there and try to get a job at the Elite. Stable boy, waiter, whatever's open. It'll give us a chance to check up on this Brick from the inside for a few days."

Mireles was ready for anything, and later in the afternoon, the Rio Kid learned that his friend had signed on as assistant wrangler at the stable yard of the Elite Hotel.

Pryor himself was keeping an eye on the shack into which he had seen Mac and Jim retire the night before. But, like others of their ilk, they slept all through the daylight hours, and it was not until eight o'clock, when dark had fallen over the wild town, that the two cronies emerged. They went to a cheap eating place, where they ordered a breakfast of ham, eggs, coffee and rolls.

Mac, because of his thin, tall figure and bony features, was easy to keep in view. After the pair of rascals had breakfast the Rio Kid watched them enter the Elite and take up stations near the gaming tables.

"Got a system, I reckon," he decided. "They watch for a winner, foller him, and knock him off."

They were obviously hard at work, and he slipped up the street, checked up, and then went inside their shack. There had been no answer to his questioning knock on the single door.

It was a one-room affair, leaning against a blank warehouse wall, and the floor was of dirt. It smelled musty. There was one little window, closed by oiled paper, a couple of cornshuck pads on the floor, a box or two to sit on, a broken bench, and dirty clothing. Several empty bottles lay in one corner where they had been tossed.

There was nothing of value in there. The Rio Kid's match, cupped in his hand, showed him the holdup men's lair to be simply a hole in which they slept.

He was about to leave when he saw a whitish

paper rectangle lying near one of the beds. It was a letter. Another match flame showed that it was postmarked St. Louis, and was addressed to Harry Mackintosh, General Delivery, Cheyenne, Wyoming T.

The Rio Kid opened it, struck another match, read the short scrawl inside:

> How ar yu, Harry old boy? It's gettin' hot here. May be I'll see you in Cheyenne. Is it good pickins there, old friend? No good here no more. Write me how it is, Harry. Yur friend,
>
> Rod Philips

The Rio Kid put the letter back, reconnoitered, and left the shack.

"Might as well make a stab at it," he thought, and headed for the Elite.

Mac and Jim were still there, watching for a new victim. The Rio Kid walked straight up to the cadaverous-faced Mackintosh.

"Hullo, Mac," he said. "How's things?"

THE bony-faced man started, staring into the Rio Kid's smiling face. He was wary, and plainly a dangerous antagonist. He wore a six-shooter, and no doubt other weapons were hidden beneath his black coat. Nearby was his partner, Jim, who turned toward them, coming at the Rio Kid from another angle in case his friend needed help.

"You talkin' to me, mister?" growled Mac,

ready for trouble. A bony hand dangled close to the six-gun stock.

"Yeah, I'd have known yuh anywheres, Mac, after Rod Philips told me about yuh." The Rio Kid nodded pleasantly. He winked. "Let's have a drink. I'm new in Cheyenne."

The keen Rio Kid, who could have beaten Mac to the draw if necessary, noted that the fellow relaxed at mention of Rod Philips. He turned and led the way to a table. Mac came after him, sat down and looked at him as Pryor ordered drinks.

"How'd yuh savvy me, just from what Rod told yuh?" Mac asked.

"I picked yuh out, Mac, but just to be shore I waited till I heard a bartender call yuh 'Mac.' You needn't worry. I worked with Rod for a while in St. Looey, and I'm all right."

Mac was interested. "How's old Rod? The son-of-a-gun! I had a letter from him last week, said he might be out hisself."

"That's right. It's a question how much longer things hold up for him back there." The Rio Kid gave a grave professional nod.

The boy brought the drinks, and Pryor paid the score.

"Help yoreself, Mac. On me, all the way."

"*Bueno.* I'm broke, I warn yuh. I shore need a drink."

Such robbers, thought the Rio Kid, were doubly fools. They stole large sums of money, but they were habitually broke, losing their evil gains at the gambling tables. The Rio Kid knew St. Louis, and Mac was eager to talk on his own, his tongue loosened by the apparently bona-fide introduction. He signaled his partner, Jim, who came over and had a couple of drinks.

"My friend Dave Burns, from St. Looey, Jim," said Mac, giving the name which the Rio Kid had had ready. "Friend of old Rod's."

Jim was ready to drink, too. He sat down saying little, and listening to the talk. The Rio Kid ordered another bottle brought over before they had finished the first. He managed to turn the talk from St. Louis to Cheyenne by simulating a stranger's interest in the settlement. "What yuh been doin'?" asked Mac. "Same as Rod?"

"Oh, I dabbled some in it." The Rio Kid nodded. "I'm sort of a jack-of-all-trades, Mac, come right down to it. Lately I fooled with cattle, even."

"Too much work involved," said Mac. "Me and Jim like to take it easy."

About them hummed the big saloon. Music banged tinnily away while the shuffle of boots and slippered feet kept time in the dance hall. They could talk across the table without being overheard, and the red whisky began having its effect, even upon Mackintosh. The tall man was the dominant partner of the team. Jim had little to say, and took his drink silently, glumly.

"Yuh reckon I could get along here for a while, Mac?" inquired the Rio Kid, in his role as a shady character. "This town looks like good pickin's."

" 'Looks like it'!" Red specks showed in the pupils of Mac's eyes and he blinked. He was feeling sorry for himself. "True enough, and plenty of work for us in Cheyenne, plenty. We was doin' fine. Then what happens?"

Mac lost the train of his speech as he hiccuped. He leaned his cheek on his hand and hitched his chair closer, a bony finger waggling in the Rio Kid's face.

"This ain't a free town, take it from one who savvies," he said mournfully. "Yuh ask my advice? Well, I'll give it straight to a pard of old Rod's. Don't pull any jobs in these parts. It don't pay."

"How so? The law too lively?"

"Shucks!" There was contempt in Mac's voice. "Who cares about the lawmen in these places? Yuh got to pay a percentage here, that's what the trouble is. If yuh don't play with the big muckamucks yuh'll wake up able to see the dancers through yore own skull. Me'n Jim do all right and take in a bit of change. Then what? We got to pay our profits to— Well, it's brutal, it's killin' me." He was sorry for himself and tears stood in his bleary eyes.

His partner touched his arm. "Hey, Mac, take it easy. We got to go to work later."

"Work, work, work! Man ain't got time to enjoy hisself at all."

But Mackintosh heeded his partner's warning and, finishing his latest glass, rose and held out his hand.

"See yuh around, boy. Me'n Jim got to be sashayin'."

Mac winked at the Rio Kid knowingly.

CHAPTER VII
The Recruit

MAC DID not offer to take the Rio Kid along. He and his partner, Jim, had enough natural cunning to avoid complications, even though "Old Rod" had vouched for the visitor to Cheyenne.

Jim and Mac left the Elite—probably, thought the Rio Kid, because they did not wish him to see them pick out a victim for their evening's attentions. He could not trail them too closely. He saw them enter another gambling house down the street, and he did not see them again until the following evening.

During that time there had been five armed robberies, and one man had been slugged so viciously that his skull was fractured. The Rio Kid learned that the next day. When he waved to Mackintosh and his partner at the Elite that night, he already had learned that they had money, and he was fairly sure that one of the crimes committed the previous night could be laid to the pair.

Cheyenne was red-hot. There were thousands coming and going, men with get-rich-quick schemes, with highest hopes, every individual intent on his own affairs, not wanting to be bothered by others. Gold miners, prospectors, meant to sneak into the Black Hills.

Some others were smugglers, running contraband liquor and weapons to the Sioux.

The Rio Kid wondered if he had wasted his time with Mackintosh and Jim, for it looked as if the two had no intention of taking him in with them. They exchanged greetings, and bought a drink at the bar. As they were going out, Mac said:

"Listen. I spoke to a friend about you, told him yuh're good at cattle. Said he'd keep yuh in mind if anything come up."

"Obliged, Mac," said Dave Burns, from St. Looey. "I'll be around."

Mireles met the Rio Kid at the livery stable, secretly, as they had agreed upon in case the Mexican had anything important to tell.

"Zey plan somesing beeg, General," Celestino insisted. "Ees cattle, I theenk. Zey hav' man-ee hombres to come but I cannot go too close."

"Plannin' to rustle a herd, most likely," said the Rio Kid thoughtfully. "The outlaw chiefs

68

in this pueblo control everything. See if yuh can pick up anything more on it."

Celestino was working in the Elite stable yard. He had good opportunities to observe the red-headed man, whose name was Brick Lowndes. Lowndes had many contacts who came and went, no doubt a large percentage of them paying for the privilege of garnering loot in Cheyenne.

That night the Rio Kid contacted Mackintosh again. He had decided to push his luck, because the bony man did not seem to be of use anyway.

"My funds are gettin' low, Mac," he complained. "Ain't there anything yuh can do for me?"

Mackintosh put a hearty hand on his shoulder, slapped his back.

"I reckon I can help out, boy," he said expansively. "I just heard of a little job. It'll take hard ridin' and mebbe some shootin'. Yuh game?"

"Shore I'm game. What is it—cattle?"

Mackintosh nodded. "It ain't permanent—just two, three days. Five a day and grub. Yuh got to furnish yore own hoss, and ammunition. If yuh do good, though, yuh might work into somethin' better."

"I got a good amount and enough bullets to make count," assured the Rio Kid. "Who do I see?"

"C'mon. I'll introduce yuh."

The long-legged killer led the Rio Kid through the crowded bar—they had been drinking in the Elite that evening—and to the back hallway. It was Brick Lowndes to whom the bony outlaw escorted the Rio Kid.

"Hyah, Brick," said Mackintosh with a heartiness which did not entirely disguise fear and respect. "Brought yuh that recruit—the young feller I spoke of. I can guarantee him all the way."

Brick Lowndes slouched back in a chair, his spurred boots on the round table, a glass in his left hand, a smoking cigar butt in blunt teeth. The Rio Kid knew how such gentry as he was imitating behaved, and Brick's mien was tough, assured as the best—or worst—of them. He stared, and the Rio Kid felt the fierce green eyes appraising him. The squashed nose twitched like a rabbit's.

There were two others present, men who had been drinking with Lowndes. One of them was a supple, dark-skinned fellow in a black suit and white shirt. The other was an elegantly dressed man in a checked suit perfectly fitting his large, well-made body. A diamond flashed from his ring, and his stickpin, set crosswise in his snow-white stock, was a large, genuine pearl in a yellow gold setting. His black boots were fine, shining with polish. His strong jaw and lower cheeks were covered by a carefully trimmed beard, but above this growth showed the pits remaining after smallpox. Despite Brick

70

Lowndes' obvious power, the fellow with the beard drew the Rio Kid's eyes. He sensed a strong character, a ruthless antagonist, and struggled to preserve the correct manner.

"You can shoot, mister?" asked Lowndes.

"Yes, sir. Anyway at all."

"Ever handle wet cattle?"

THE Rio Kid shrugged, nodded. He could never have made it with Brick, without such a recommendation as Mackintosh supplied, and now he was glad he had gone to such trouble to cultivate the bony thief and killer.

After Lowndes had questioned the recruit, he looked quickly at the bearded man. There was the deepest deference in the red-headed man's usually insolent, bold eyes. The well-dressed fellow gave an almost imperceptible nod, and Brick turned back to the Rio Kid.

"I'll give yuh a trial, Burns," he said. "There's two, three days' work at five per day, but if yuh do all right I'll have more for yuh later."

"*Bueno*. When yuh want me?"

"We're startin' after dark tomorrer but we don't all leave town together. I'll meet yuh on Crow Crik, at the upper ford. Yuh savvy where it is?"

"Yeah, I savvy."

"Be there on time. I ain't waitin' for anybody. Keep yore lip buttoned and don't show up full of red-eye or yuh won't go."

"Yes, sir."

71

Lowndes pointed at the dark-skinned man, who had the aspect and manner of a professional gambler.

"This here is Aloysius, my pardner, Burns," he said. "Yuh can take orders from him as yuh would from me."

Mackintosh was awaiting the Rio Kid outside.

"How'd yuh make out?" asked the bony man.

"Fine, I reckon. I got a little job, and I'm obliged, Mac."

"Don't mention it. Any pard of old Rod's is worth his salt."

"That feller by Brick is Aloysius, his pardner, he told me," said the Rio Kid. "I was s'prised they'd let anybody else hear what was said, though—you savvy, that hombre with the beard on him."

"You don't have to worry. That's Hansinger. He runs a real estate shebang in town, but he's a good friend of Brick's. Gambles with 'em a lot." Mackintosh winked. "Them buzzards take no chances."

"Hansinger," the Rio Kid repeated. He had been deeply impressed by the bearded man. A shrewd judge of character, he would have classed Hansinger as more dangerous than either Lowndes or Aloysius, tough as they were. . . .

After dark the following day, the Rio Kid rode Saber out to the upper ford on Crow Creek. Behind him, Cheyenne was lighting oil lamps and candles, beginning to glow yellow over the rising plains. The air was rare, cool, and the stream purled in its rocky bed.

There were riders around the ford, for the Rio Kid could see the glow of cigars and cigarettes. In the dim light, he made out a number of men, some sitting their saddles, others dismounted by their horses. No one had anything to say, except one or two who had friends along and who talked in low voices. The Rio Kid counted thirty-three men besides himself at the rendezvous. Brick Lowndes appeared half an hour later. He came along, riding a fine black gelding with a flowing mane and tail and a white blotch on its forehead. He moved around, checking up on his men. When he saw the Rio Kid, he nodded.

"Glad yuh're here, Burns," he said. "We're ridin' now."

He signaled them to follow, and led the way, taking a trail on the north bank of the creek.

It was a monotonous run, most of it uphill. Now and then the riders paused to rest the horses, smoke and drink from canteens. Hard eyes glowed in the moonlight.

They kept going all night, and did not stop for any length of time until the sky behind them was turning grayish. The Rio Kid decided they had come thirty miles or more from town, and hills rose about, interspersed with rolling, grassy plains. In a pine woods on a height, Lowndes pulled up, and called them together.

"Here we are boys," he said. He had a masterful way, a leader's surety of manner, of speech. "Unsaddle, picket yore hosses. I want yuh to get some shut-eye. Yuh can eat, drink and smoke, but hide yore match flares behind them boulders, savvy? No cookin'. And keep it quiet."

They made a bivouac, screened by the woods and by the rocks and contours of the land. The party partook of jerky, hard biscuits and water, then laid down to rest.

The sun rose over the vast wilds. Birds and insects flitted through the thickets, and a warming wind came up. But Lowndes stayed asleep under his blanket, snoring gently. He had several henchmen with him, men he trusted to the hilt.

In the daylight, the Rio Kid could make out the features of the gunmen clearly. They wore leather and Stetsons, and were armored with six-shooters. Some had hard eyes, tough jaws, but others did not show they were outlaws. They might have been a crew from some large ranch.

BEFORE noon, Lowndes roused, swearing as he rubbed his eyes. He had a drink from a spiked canteen, ate some dried meat and a piece of hardtack, and wiped his ugly mouth on the back of his bare forearm.

"Let's take a look at the set-up, Sam," he said to one of his men.

The Sam to whom he spoke was a small, wiry man of around forty. He wore dark leather, and his skin was bronzed and dried out from the sun and winds. He had a cud of tobacco in one cheek, and his legs were as bowed as a ring.

Brick took a pair of field-glasses, then he and Sam moved to the top of the crest and lay down. The Rio Kid could see the red-haired boss adjusting the binoculars and for a time, Lowndes studied objects beyond the crest, to the west.

After a while Brick turned and beckoned. His most trusted men led the others up to the crest, but cautioned them to keep low so they would not be seen. Lowndes spoke to them in a normal tone.

"Want every man to study the ground," he said. "Take a good look."

The Rio Kid chose a flat boulder, peering around it in approved scouting style. He saw that along the bank of a small stream stood a wagon camp, with the vehicles drawn into a circle. There were people down there, women and men and children. Distantly they caught the lowing of cattle and dust rose beyond the camp site.

"They got a big herd over there, fellers," Lowndes said, "and that's what we're after. Spiky Sam here's in charge of runnin' the cows off, and what he says goes. I'm takin' half the men with me, and we're goin' to keep them camp folks busy tonight while Sam and the other bunch run off the beef. We'll stampede their hosses first and dust 'em with slugs enough so's they won't want to trail us. By that time Sam'll have the herd out of their reach."

"Who are they, Brick?" asked a gunman curiously.

"Bunch of Texans just off the trail and green in these parts. It'll be a cinch."

The Rio Kid held himself in. He recognized the wagons and the layout, thought even now some of the figures familiar. They were Colonel Gus Jennings' people, whom he had met when he had found a sanctuary for Frank Warren!

CHAPTER VIII
Rustler Trek

FOR a moment the Rio Kid felt almost stunned. He had been aware that Brick Lowndes, with his powerful gang, would have victims in mind when they had started the ride, but it had been impersonal then. Now he knew the folks the rustler crew meant to hit. And he knew that loss of the herd would ruin the Texans, to say nothing of the fact that some would be shot, perhaps killed. He searched his brain for a way to give them warning.

"Spiky Sam" had binoculars, too, and had been using them.

"Looks like they have a wounded hombre there, Brick," he said to Lowndes. "They're carryin' him from a wagon into the sunlight."

Brick shifted his glasses a bit, studying the scene. He craned his neck as though the few more inches might make details clearer.

"I can't see him so well," he complained. "Wish they'd turn him around."

With the naked eye, the Rio Kid could see two men carrying a figure on a stretched blanket. They laid the invalid in the warmth of the morning sun. By the sick man hovered a girl in a blue dress.

"That'll be Jennings' girl, Alyse," thought Pryor.

The girl in the blue dress drew the attention of Brick Lowndes, and he looked at her for long through the field glasses.

"Seems like she's in love with that sick hombre," Lowndes remarked. "She's awful tender with him. I'm wondering if it's a man-and-wife situation."

"Mebbe the sick gent has the cholera," Spiky remarked. That being the case we would do better to leave the stock alone. Cholera sticks right along with cows. I've heard tell it's spread through lice. You got to burn all the clothing and the blankets to stop a plague. I'm not any too anxious to run into any of that disease."

Brick Lowndes lowered his glasses.

"Yuh always are carpin' about something," he roared. "There ain't no cholera in that outfit. There ain't been none around here for years. Are yuh gettin' cold feet about raidin' that outfit, Spiky?"

"No, I ain't gettin' cold feet," Spiky said quickly. "I jest want to make sure."

Brick Lowndes raised his glasses again.

"That hombre on the ground ain't sick with disease," Lowndes said. "He's hurt. I'd say he had been shot. How would he get shot? If them settlers had a fight, then they'll be watchin' out for something to happen."

Lowndes uttered a terrible oath, in excitement.

"Good glory, Spiky, yuh savvy who that is on the blanket? I believe it's that printer sidewinder, Frank Warren!"

The Rio Kid knew that Lowndes was correct. Alyse was propping up the invalid. She had brought a bowl of food and knelt beside him, feeding him.

"Reckon that is Warren, Brick," said Spiky Sam, excited himself. "Ain't there a five-hundred-dollar bonus for his hide?"

"Right. Why, Hansinger'd rather have Warren than all the herds in Texas! What plumb luck! We'll finish off Warren tonight when we hit their camp. He must've rode out of Cheyenne durin' the fire and these fools picked him up on the plains and fetched him here. Small world, huh?"

Hansinger, thought the Rio Kid. That name brought to his mind the man with the spade beard. Hansinger was with them, in spirit, Brick Lowndes as the man's physical representative.

Brick could scarcely contain himself. He chewed savagely on a cold cigar and muttered over and over what he meant to do to Frank Warren and those who had aided him.

"They must've had him in one of the wagons while I was spyin' 'em out," observed Spiky Sam. "I'll admit I had my eyes more on them cows than on the owners, though. Its a golden chance, right now, Brick, to run off the herd. They ain't split up yet, as they mean to do soon."

"They own this land?" asked Lowndes.

"Yeah, I believe so. I asked around some, and this here Colonel Jennings, their leader, was here last spring and picked out this range. It's fine grazin' hereabouts. They intend buildin' homes and stickin'. Right now they're all workin' together till they're set up."

"How far south is the railroad line?" asked Brick.

"Oh, a good thirty miles, I'd say. Not too much of a drive, though, if they want to ship cattle east or to Californy."

Spiky Sam was expert at cattle. It was he who, always hunting for such chances, had observed the Texans and laid out the job, then reported to Lowndes.

"They're into everything, that's plain," thought the Rio Kid. "Robb'ry, rustlin', and gamblin'. Mac was right. Lowndes and the gang take a split on all outlawry in the region."

There was plenty of market for beef, in Cheyenne itself, at the railroad camps, or they could run into Utah and dispose of the stolen cows around Salt Lake City. All they needed was a start.

The Rio Kid, too, could hardly contain himself, but for a different reason than Lowndes. He must warn Jennings and try to save the Texans and Warren from the gunmen. With this prime purpose in mind he watched throughout the afternoon for the slightest opportunity to slip away, but it was impossible. The horses were unsaddled and picketed under guard, and he would have had to ride off in plain sight. They would order him back, shoot him if he refused to obey. The shots would be lost in the open spaces or, if heard dimly at the camp, would be ascribed to hunters.

The hours slipped away, and around six P.M. they ate another cold meal from their saddlebags.

"Get goin' and place yore men in position, Spiky," Brick Lowndes said to Spiky Sam, then. "Ride behind that line of ridges and yuh'll be hid all right."

Spiky Sam picked his crew. Lowndes nudged him, said something in his ear, and Spiky pointed at the Rio Kid.

"You—what's yore handle?"

"Burns—Dave Burns."

"Come along with me. I understand yuh're good at handlin' cows. We'll give yuh a chance to prove it tonight. . . . Now, boys, we're ridin' pardners, savvy? I want yuh to pair off, and one help the other in case of trouble. They don't

81

leave but four or five night herders out there, and Brick'll see to it no help comes from the camp. We're goin' to run the herd straight south and then swing back east till we hit the plains. From then on it'll be a snap."

ABOUT sixteen rustlers were going with Spiky Sam. The wiry little chief spoke to one of them, an older fellow with a round head and a stocky body. He was called Kinny, and he had had little to say during the day. Instead, he had dozed and taken it easy, waiting for the darkness. He strolled over to the Rio Kid.

"Boss says we're to pair up, Burns. Let's get saddled."

"Fine. That suits me, Kinny."

Pryor appraised Kinny more carefully now. The man had a steady eye and a confident air. He was experienced, and knew how to handle horses, and from the way he wore his guns, the Rio Kid decided that Kinny would not be an easy person to fool.

Playing out his role as new to the gang and eager to make his mark and show how good he was, the Rio Kid checked his pistols, saddled up the mouse-colored dun, and acted as a rustler should when getting ready to go to work.

Kinny was watching him all the time, although not openly. He was judging the new hand to see if he knew his business. None of them were suspicious of the Rio Kid, for the guarantee of Harry Mackintosh had fooled Lowndes, and no one would have been brought along if there had been any doubt about him. But they wish to see how he would conduct himself under fire and in action.

Now Spiky Sam's gang had their mounts saddled and weapons loaded and checked. They waited silently as Sam had a last word with Brick Lowndes. Then the wiry little rustler took the lead and they wound off to the northwest but soon straightened out, keeping a series of ridges and long hills between them and the camp of the Texans. The way was rocky enough or grassed so that no dust rose which might warn Jennings that a large band was approaching.

Kinny rode just to the rear of the Rio Kid, either by accident or design. They were in the middle of the procession. Spiky Sam knew the surroundings and landmarks, and for an hour they slowly wound through the beflowered, gorgeous wilds, working around to the west side of the Texas herd. The sun was a huge red ball, glaring before them in the intense sky. It was making ready to disappear behind the distant Rockies.

The Rio Kid waited for nightfall. Then he must seize any slim opportunity to shake off Kinny and the others, so as to carry the grave warning to Jennings. From what he had overheard, the attack was to begin at midnight, and

Spiky Sam would synchronize his actions with Lowndes' blow at the sleeping encampment.

At last darkness fell over Wyoming. Stars could now be seen, and a pale moon was coming into view, to give them enough light to work by. Once Lowndes immobilized Jennings and the main bunch, there would be little difficulty. They would have to reckon only with a few night guards around the herd.

The rustlers spoke little and then in lowered voices, although there was no chance of speech being overheard, from such a distance, by their luckless victims. The Rio Kid was in a closed column of horsemen, and the way they were traveling now was narrow, with steep, wooded banks rising on either side.

He was not familiar with this section of the country, and could only guess at the location of Jennings' camp. It must be somewhere south, and a mile or two east, he thought. He knew that the Texans were east of the herd's bedding grounds.

As he slowed a bit, Kinny's mustang bumped Saber, and the dun turned and bit at the other horse. Saber's temper was short with other animals.

"Keep goin', Bub," ordered Kinny in a low voice.

Spiky Sam swore, as he looked back at the slight disturbance.

"Keep it quiet, boys," he ordered, and the word was passed along the line.

Suddenly the hills seemed to melt away on both sides. Spiky Sam checked the advance and dismounted.

"Stick here and keep it quiet," he whispered, and stole away around a bulging rock.

Soon he was back, and he had them all come close around him.

"It's all right," he reported. "The herd's there, bedded or grazin'. There's only a handful of men with the cows. We're goin' to spread around in a half circle, base here and curve on the west, savvy? I'll be in the center. When yuh hear my 'Wa-hoo' yell everybody charge in and take care of any guards yuh run onto. Then we'll turn and drive south. There won't be any trouble from the camp side. If one or two get away from us, they'll meet up with Brick's gang. C'mon—spread out, and we'll wait till the right time comes."

Sweat prickled on the Rio Kid's flesh. He could hardly hold himself back from dashing away in a desperate attempt to carry the word to Jennings. He did not like to throw away the inside advantage he had with Lowndes' powerful Cheyenne outfit, for Dodge had sent him to smash them. But he could not allow the cruel attack to succeed.

PAIRS of riders were being started off, to take up their positions. Kinny and the Rio Kid were sixth among the twosomes, and they walked their horses out, past the contour which cut off the view.

"There she is," said Kinny, as they drew up on a shelflike meadow overlooking a large, grassy plain.

Dark shadows blotched the rolling plain. They were batches of Texas steers, some lying down, chewing their cud, others up grazing. The cattle were quiet in the calm, cool night. The Rio Kid saw that the space was filled with animals. He could not pick out any of the herders yet, however.

To the east, the sides of the basin rose, but a blacker section told him there must be a way through. As his keen, trained eyes swept the placid scene, he saw a faint reddish glow not far from the pass, and concluded that must be the dying camp-fire of the Texans.

He had to keep cool, for he did not wish Kinny to think he was excited over anything.

"Looks easy enough, Kinny," he whispered.

"Don't worry," answered Kinny. "It'll go like clockwork. When yuh work with fellers like Brick and Spiky yuh don't need to fuss. They're good."

"About an hour, I reckon, before Brick hits, huh?"

"Little more, I'd say, till midnight. I'd put it at ten-thirty now. Better muzzle that loco brute of yores so's he don't let out a shriek or somethin'. C'mon—get down."

Kinny had the advantage of him still. Not

once had the rustler got in front of him. The man was naturally cautious, and he had been told to watch the new recruit. But as he dismounted his horse swung half-way around, and Kinny took off his bandanna, using both hands as he began tying the cloth around his mustang's muzzle. Just for a few seconds, as he was busy with the kerchief, his reins on the ground, was Kinny's back to the Rio Kid.

"Now or never!" thought Pryor.

He slugged Kinny from behind with an expert's blow, and the stocky rustler folded up with a grunt at his horse's forehoofs. The Rio Kid was on him then, and in a second had him tied and gagged. He rolled Kinny into a grassy hollow, picketed the horse so it would not stray, and started off, leading Saber.

Shadows were cast by the contours and by high brush growth on the ridge, and he made use of them. He must not let the rustlers see him as he moved toward the camp.

Twenty minutes later he was through the black gap, and stopped as he saw the ghostly shapes of the big wagons drawn up by the stream. The red embers of the fire glowed as the night wind gusted up. A man was sitting on a rock, some yards from the fire. He was leaning on his rifle—a sentry taking his turn to guard against chance Indian attacks. The Rio Kid could see his slumped figure, and as he listened he heard the man cough.

Dropping his reins, the Rio Kid slipped across

the brook on foot and approached the sentry, who suddenly whirled, rifle rising.

"Who's that?" he challenged.

"A friend—the Rio Kid. Keep it quiet."

"The Rio Kid! Say, I'm Ed McNeill. I remember you on the trail."

The Rio Kid recalled Ed McNeill, son of Major McNeill, one of Gus Jennings' men.

"*Bueno,* Ed," he said. "Come out of that light so's we can pow-wow. I got mighty important news."

Ed stepped over, staring at the lithe Rio Kid in the dimness.

"What's up?" he whispered.

"There's a bunch of rustlers after yore herd and they mean to attack yore camp, Ed. Where's the Colonel?"

"Sleepin' right over heah."

"Take me to him," ordered the Rio Kid. "We got to rouse everybody pronto."

CHAPTER IX
Night Fight

JENNINGS was asleep under his wagon, in which his wife and Alyse made their beds. A low moan startled the Rio Kid as he followed Ed McNeill.

"That's Warren, the young feller you fetched in," the Texan said. "He's still out of his haid, and he ain't too strong. We have to tie him down at night or he gets up and staggers around yellin' murder."

Colonel Gus Jennings roused quickly, as McNeill and the Rio Kid crawled under the wagon to shake him awake.

"Yore camp's goin' to be hit within the hour, Colonel," reported Pryor bluntly. "We better get riflemen set, and yuh'll have to snake some reinforcements out to guard yore herd."

"Hey, what's this? Huh?'" Jennings was dazed at the sudden alarm, and his voice rose.

"Keep it quiet, Colonel," warned the Rio Kid. "We want to s'prise 'em."

He gave Jennings a quick account of the enemy plan.

"Wake yore boys quiet-like," he advised them. "Have 'em loaded up and hid under the wagons. Yuh got a tough gang to fight off."

Under the Rio Kid's deft orders the camp was awakened with little fuss. Men crawled from spot to spot, shaking friends, cautioning each to keep silent, to load his guns and make ready for a battle. The wagons threw long black shadows which they utilized in moving about.

Major McNeill, with eight fighters, stole away through the gap, afoot, to help the herd guards fight off Spiky Sam and his rustlers.

The Rio Kid crouched beside a heavy wagon tongue, on the east side of the encampment. All was quiet behind him, in the alerted camp. A blotch of woods to the east kept him straining his eyes that way.

They had been ready but a short time when he caught a movement, the dark shadow of a man stealthily emerging from the trees and coming toward the camp. But there were more and more figures. Some, half-crouched, were to the left and right of the first he had been able to spy—Brick Lowndes' tried killers, pushing in to deal with the supposedly sleeping Texans.

The horses of the ranchers were in a corral

made from lariats stretched around trees, this temporary pen enclosing a section of the stream so the mustangs could drink. Lowndes meant to stampede them, run off what he could, and leave the shocked, bleeding victims high and dry.

The gunmen made hardly any sound as they stole in on the camp. The watching men could now make out the stealthy figures, even the glint of the moonlight on rifle barrel here and there. They were disposed in a semi-circle, so as to sweep up the whole camp and pin the Texans against the brook and the rising ground beyond.

It was eerie, waiting, holding it, watching the desperadoes come in for the kill. The Rio Kid was to give the signal to fire, but he intended to let the enemy get so close that the marksmen could not possibly miss as the half circle drew in.

A heavy Sharps boomed, flaring its charge to his left. Someone had fired ahead of time at the enemy.

The Rio Kid was irritated. He would have given the attackers a few more seconds, perhaps a full minute before he let go. But the die was cast and he shouted, "Fire, Texas!" and opened up with his carbine.

A deafening blast roared from the guns of the cowmen, who were hidden under their wagons or by the drop of the brook bed. The enemy line stopped, and some went to their knees.

"Let go, cuss it!"

A frantic order issued from Brick Lowndes, who was well to the rear as he pushed his men in.

Sparking guns answered the Texans. Bullets clipped the steel-shod wheels or cut chunks of wood from spokes. Other slugs shrieked through the night air to plug into the ground. Men began cursing, shouting defiance.

"Wa-hoo! Wa-hoo!"

From the west, where the herd lay, Spiky Sam's ear-splitting shrieks sounded with a frantic insistence, and gunfire could be heard. The Rio Kid grinned to himself as he thought how surprised Spiky was going to be.

But he had plenty to do where he was. Stunned for a moment by the sudden fire, the Lowndes fighters rallied. They still believed they could overrun the camp, and Brick was stinging them on. They jumped up, whooping hoarsely, shooting full guns, as they charged.

YELLING, shooting demons rushed the heart of the wagon camp. The Rio Kid, Colts going full-blast, fought with a desperate fury, and the Texans held well, not panicking, handling their weapons like trained soldiers.

The clash of battle rang over the scene. A cowman close to Pryor threw up his hands and fell over on his face. Another was crying out from a wound. Heavy weapons roared, flamed in the night.

But the attackers had been surprised, as they had hoped to surprise the cowmen. Instead of a sleeping camp, easy meat for their guns, and dread confusion, they had run into stinging, well-directed fire, and they did not like it. At the ends, several turned off, to hunt cover, hearing the hot lead close about their ears. In the center, several had been hit, and two lay silent forever where they had fallen.

The Rio Kid, who could judge a fight, sensed that the turning point had come, and he was right. The enemy surged up, reached the break, and disintegrated into a panicky mob, then into individuals, every one seeking only to escape. They turned to run, diving off, each man intent on getting away. Nothing could stop them, and the rancher bullets only made them run faster.

Within a few more seconds, the battle was over, won by the welcoming committee which the Rio Kid had organized.

"Let's get after 'em!" bellowed Gus Jennings, leaping out from his wagon.

Enthusiastic Texans were popping up from every bit of cover, from behind wagon wheels and rocks, ready to follow Jennings.

"Hold it!" called the Rio Kid.

The enemy had entered the black woods, as they rushed to pick up their mustangs. They would be dangerous if pressed. Better to let them go, for they could not be checked.

As the fury died off at camp, they could hear shouts and guns more clearly from the west, where the herd lay. Cattle bellowed.

"Let's get over and help protect the herd," said the Rio Kid to Jennings. "Leave a few men on guard here."

Spiky Sam, still unaware of the fiasco at the camp where Brick was supposed to be cleaning out the Texans, was trying desperately to beat back the defenders of the cattle. He had run into a hornet's nest, just as Lowndes had. There seemed to be guards everywhere, and bullets stung back the rustlers.

The wiry little rustler chief, cursing at the top of his voice, was off to the right of the gap. He saw the dark shapes of the Rio Kid and a bunch of the Texans as they hurried over, and mistook them for the reinforcements he was waiting for.

"Hey, Brick—hustle it up!" he yelled. "We're bein' cut to pieces!"

Spiky Sam, guns flaring at the cowboys, dashed right up to them before he suddenly realized his error.

"Throw down, Sam!" ordered the Rio Kid.

The rustler would not surrender. He fired hastily at the Stetson on the Rio Kid's head, and the slug whipped the felt. The Rio Kid and Gus Jennings poured lead into Spiky Sam, and the cattle thief was knocked off his feet by the heavy bullets, dead as he landed.

The steers were frightened by the flashing guns and the booming reports. They were milling, churning around and bellowing, and suddenly the stampede began. Heavy, blinded animals charged forward and nothing could stop the rush. They broke through the thin lines, and men scattered before them, unable to check the stampede. Dust rose thick, and the thunder of hoofs shook the earth.

Spiky Sam's men, their leader gone, were also stampeding, picking up their horses, riding away from there.

The Rio Kid and his friends hunted for foes in the dark. Some cowboys mounted to follow the cows and be ready when dawn came to turn the herd.

Brick Lowndes and his bunch had left, headed back to Cheyenne in a wild retreat, every man for himself.

A little while later, the Rio Kid squatted by the stirred-up fire, drinking hot coffee with Gus Jennings and a circle of the Texans, as they reviewed the fight.

"It would have been a lot different if you hadn't been here, Rio Kid," Jennings said gravely. "We'd have lost more'n one killed and three wounded if you hadn't fetched the warnin'."

"Drew, you went off half-cocked," growled an older rancher, Vern Lytle. "If yuh'd held

95

till the Rio Kid give the signal, we'd mebbe not have lost anybody. They'd have panicked and been cut to ribbons. I'm on'y tellin' yuh so's yuh'll obey orders next time, savvy? Yuh're young and yuh ain't had battle experience, but remember."

Lytle had been next to Drew Young, the curly-haired young fire-eater. Young's eyes flamed at the criticism. He didn't like it. "Shucks!" he said gruffly. "I had a clean bead on one and I had to let go. Reckon I fought all right."

"Yeah, yuh done fine for a younker," said Jennings heartily.

ALYSE, in a calico dress and with her hair braided in pigtails, tied on the ends with blue ribbons, was helping her mother who had charge of caring for the wounded. One man had died, another had been hit in the leg and was suffering a good deal. Two had flesh wounds, while many had burns and scratches.

The other women served a meal to the men, and everybody rested for a time. The Rio Kid was glad of the respite, for with the job he was doing for General Dodge in his mind, he knew he must return to Cheyenne as speedily as possible.

As the first touch of grayness came in the east, Colonel Jennings sent a crew out to help hunt up the cows and begin driving the scattered cattle back to the vicinity of camp.

Jennings rode with the Rio Kid to the bedding-grounds, as Pryor sought the spot where he had left Kinny, the tough rustler he had bested the night before.

Kinny lay, stiff as a board, in the grassy hollow up on the brush-screened shelf to the northwest of the plain where the cattle had been held. His horse, panicked by the battle so close at hand, had pulled loose and run away during the darkness.

"Dead as a doornail!" exclaimed Jennings, who had dismounted, and slid down into the circular pot-hole in which the Rio Kid had rolled the tied, gagged rustler.

The rancher was a heavy man. His boot broke through the earth and he sank to his knee, swearing as he sought to recover his balance. Then he bent over Kinny, and rolled the dead man over on his back.

CHAPTER X
The Strike

THE RIO KID stood on the edge of the hollow, staring at the rustler. Kinny's face was purple over the gag, and Jennings loosened the bandanna and pulled it off. The features were swollen and discolored.

"You must've gagged him too tight, Rio Kid," said Jennings. "He smothered to death. Well, that's one rustler won't waste rope." He stopped talking abruptly, and a troubled look came over his face. He brushed imaginary cobwebs from his eyes. "Poof! Reckon—I went too hard—last night." His speech was thick.

The Rio Kid was alarmed. He thought perhaps the florid, heavy cowman was having a heart attack. Jennings was squatted down. He put out a hand to steady himself, then he silently keeled over on his side and lay across Kinny's body.

"Jennings! What in all creation!"

The Rio Kid seized the limp arm and dragged the heavy rancher from the hole.

Now he glimpsed the crevice in the rock under the shallow layer of earth and vegetation through which Jennings' boot had gone when he had jumped down into the hollow. But he was busy checking Jennings. He laid the rancher out and began fanning the man's face with his hat.

Jennings was breathing in gasps that seemed tortured. His face had turned sickly, bluish under the thick coat of tan. As the Rio Kid worked over him, however, his breathing became more regular and after a few minutes he opened his eyes, licking at his lips with his tongue, and swearing weakly.

"What hit me? Huh?"

"Yuh fainted, Jennings," said the Rio Kid.

"Fainted? Me? Say, I ain't ever fainted. I got a heart like a two-year-old bull!"

He sat up, ashamed of the momentary weakness he had shown.

A faint breeze touched them as the morning wind came up. A pink area in the eastern sky heralded the sun's coming. The Rio Kid sat on his haunches, reaching for his tobacco and papers.

He fixed a cigarette and handed the makings to Jennings.

Then he lighted a match.

There was a startling, whooshing sound, and

the Rio Kid felt his face go hot. Both men rolled away. Bluish flame spurted from the pot-hole, and the dead Kinny's clothing began to smoke.

"By Jiminy, that's a natural gas pocket!" cried the Rio Kid, first to realize what they had come upon.

"What!"

"Yeah, I'm certain. I've seen 'em in the Yellerstone and other places. C'mon—let's throw some rocks and dirt over that fire, before it gets goin'."

They worked frantically, and cut off the opening, so that the blue flame died away. The Rio Kid, his eyebrows and lashes singed, stared at the smoking hole, at the vegetation now blackened around it.

"That's what killed Kinny, not the gag!" he said. "He was lyin' over the leak all night and the gas finished him off. Yore foot goin' through the crust enlarged the hole and the gas made yuh dizzy mighty quick, Colonel."

"Cussed stuff's dangerous!" growled Jennings. "I hope there ain't much of it on our range."

"Well, usually when yuh find a little leak like this it means there's a lot of it trapped underground. But yuh'd have to have an engineer to check up. Let's go back to camp. Some of yore men can come out and bury Kinny in the hole later. I got to be goin' back to Cheyenne pronto."

The day shone over the wagon camp. Some of the men, women and children were at breakfast, others were working. Clothing was being washed in the brook, and animals were being watered.

They had buried three dead gunnies at the outskirts of the woods, and there were two more, Spiky Sam and Kinny, over at the bedding ground. Others had carried away Texas lead.

Drew Young, sullen because he had been called down, sat on a flat rock nearby. He pretended to be busy braiding a lariat, but actually he was sulking. The Rio Kid did not fancy the young man, whose temper was ungovernable. But then, he thought, "We ain't all gold pieces so everybody loves us!" He would ignore Young, unless the fellow insisted on a fight.

Sara Jennings came to her husband, staring up into his face.

"Gus, you looked peaked," she said anxiously. "Do you feel all right?"

"Oh, fine. Funny thing. We went over to look at the rustler the Rio Kid tied up last night and rolled into a pot-hole, Mother. I get down and purty soon I keel over! Yuh savvy what? It was gas, natural gas comin' out of a crack in the bedrock!"

DREW YOUNG was listening, but his eyes were on Alyse Jennings, who was standing at the rear of a big, covered wagon.

"Alyse is mighty worried about that young fellow you fetched in to us, Rio Kid," said Mrs. Jennings. "She hovers over him all day long, nursing him."

"Yeah? How is he?"

She shook her head, pursed her lips. "I can't do much more for him. If you ask me he'll never get well till that bullet is taken out from under his scalp. There's one in there, sure enough. I don't dare tamper with it, though, for fear of killing him."

"I better have a look at him."

Frank Warren lay on his blanket bed in the wagon body. His face was thin, his eyes still had that look of distress which the Rio Kid remembered. They had put clean clothes on him, and washed him, and made him as comfortable as possible. Alyse and Warren were looking at one another.

"Handsome youngster, isn't he?" said Sara Jennings. "He seems mighty decent, too. He talks pretty, even when he's out of his head."

The Rio Kid put a hand on the iron-sheathed wagon end and jumped into the vehicle where he knelt to look at Warren's head. He wished to see what the wound was like, now that the swelling had subsided. They had cut away the matted hair and cleansed the wound and Sara Jennings and Alyse had been applying warm herb poultices regularly. The lips of the wound had partially closed but there was a lump as large as a pigeon's egg under the dis-colored scalp.

Warren shrank from him, crying out:

"No—don't kill him! Don't shoot! I'll . . . go away!" He trembled violently, his wide eyes agonized. "Hansinger, you—"

"Don't be afraid, Frank. It's all right. We're your friends."

Pity was in Alyse's soft voice as she touched Warren's shaking hand and soothed his brow.

He quieted, but kept looking fearfully at the Rio Kid, and his distorted mind recognized him as a mortal enemy.

"Alyse is the only one who can quiet him when he acts that way," said Mrs. Jennings. "He calls everybody 'Hansinger.' We reckon that must be the name of the man who hurt him. Alyse takes care of the boy most of the day now. She's a good girl."

The Rio Kid agreed that Warren needed expert attention.

"Tell yuh what," he said. "I'm goin' to Cheyenne, and I'll send word to General Dodge, who ain't far away, and have him send out a surgeon. We can't run Warren to town yet. This Hansinger, Lowndes and the rest would kill him. He riled the powers-that-be in town and I figure they attacked that newspaper, killed the editor and burnt the place down—but I need more proof."

The Rio Kid and Gus Jennings walked from the wagon to speak together. Pryor had already informed the Texan that he was operating in Grenville Dodge's behalf, against the Cheyenne outlaws.

"Now, Colonel," said the Rio Kid, "you keep a regular guard, day and night, and sleep on yore guns. Hansinger and his men'll want revenge, and they seem to be determined to kill Frank Warren. Chances are Warren's a dangerous witness against 'em."

The ranchers had been on the point of splitting up the wagon camp, each one intending to settle on his section of range. But now all agreed they should stay together until the danger had passed.

Drew Young had come over to the wagon, where Alyse sat beside Frank Warren. The burning emotion in Young's eyes did not escape the Rio Kid.

"Jealous, shore enough," thought Pryor. "He's loco over Alyse and her cottonin' to Warren has drove him off the track." There could be a bad egg in every basket, he mused.

But he was pressed by the need to get on the trail of the killers controlling Cheyenne. He left Jennings and started to pick up Saber. His course took him around the big wagon where Warren and Alyse were. As he came abreast of its rear he saw Drew Young reach in, seize Warren's ankles and pull the wounded man out. He let Warren hit the ground. Warren cried out.

"He's shammin'—he ain't sick!" growled

Young, who was in a passion, his face dark with suffused blood, his eyes flaming.

Alyse was horrified. "Drew, stop it! How could you!"

"Cuss him, he's come between us. Yuh're sweet on him. I'll kill any man does that—"

"Quit it, Young!" snapped the Rio Kid. "Behave yourself."

Drew Young turned on him with a snarl. "You keep out of this or yuh'll find yoreself where Warren is," he threatened.

Drew Young's self-control had cracked. The words of hate rushed from his twisted mouth, his rage concentrating on the Rio Kid.

"It's yore doin's, Rio Kid!" he accused. "If yuh hadn't fetched this Yankee scum to our wagons there wouldn't have been any trouble at all. These fellers from Cheyenne hit us because Warren was here! I ought to blow yuh to tarnation!"

THE RIO KID was ready. He stood, feet spread, his arms hanging easily. He knew that such men as Drew Young, when in a rage, were liable to end an argument with a pistol.

"Yuh're a fool, Young," he drawled, his coolness a sharp contrast to the other man's high temper. "If yuh touch Warren again I'll beat yore head in myself, savvy?"

It was a dare and Drew Young would not back down in front of Alyse. He kicked Warren in the ribs. The injured man shrank against the big wagon wheel.

The Rio Kid's fist lashed out with a rattler's speed in striking, catching Young in the nose, staggering him. With a roar, Young dug in his high heels and charged, but the lithe Pryor sidestepped, and caught Young as he went past. It was enough to knock the man off balance, big as he was, so that he fell face down in the dirt.

Young came up on his knees. He meant to draw and fire now.

But the ruckus had drawn Gus Jennings and others. The huge rancher leaped, seized Young's arms from behind, wresting the gun from his fingers. Jennings easily lifted Young and shook him violently, punishing him with kicks.

"Yuh dumb jackass! Behave yoreself. I been watchin' you lately and yuh act loco. So yuh'd shoot the Rio Kid, the man who saved us? Get on to yore bedroll and stay there till you come to yore senses. Keep away from Alyse. Yuh ain't fit to speak to her or any decent woman."

Jennings was furious at Young's stupid savagery. He began to apologize to the Rio Kid, as Drew Young, afraid of the boss, slunk off.

The Rio Kid was not the kind to hold a grudge. A man such as Young, frustrated in love, was likely to explode.

He saddled the dun, took his leave of the Texans, and headed for Cheyenne, straight to the heart of the enemy stronghold.

CHAPTER XI
Boss of Cheyenne

ARRIVING in Cheyenne, the Rio Kid was not many hours behind Brick Lowndes. The settlement roared as usual, teeming with its heterogeneous population. In the early evening the eating places, saloons and gambling dens were beginning to buzz.

His first act, after caring for Saber, was to contact Celestino Mireles, who was delighted to see him.

"I wor-ree, General, when you do not come pronto," Celestino told him. "Senor Lowndes, he come back. He hav' wound-ed arm and go to médico for fix. He was tore, dirtee, and een ter-ri-ble tempair."

"Where's Lowndes now?"

"I theenk he go ovair to Rollins House. Firs' he sleep, aftair hees wound was fix."

"I'll go after him. But I want you to ride over with a message to General Dodge."

He had a report written out in which he informed Dodge of all he had learned, and he asked the General to hurry a surgeon out to take care of Frank Warren. Knowing he could trust his Mexican partner as he would himself, the Rio Kid handed the report to Celestino and left the stable, at the rear of the Elite, where he had met his trail partner.

He went across the street to the elegant Rollins House and, looking in through the saloon batwings, saw Brick Lowndes with Aloysius at the long bar which was crowded with merrymakers. Music was being banged from pianos and violins.

Brick's left forearm was bandaged. There were scratches and contusions on the red-head's face and head and he appeared downcast, his green eyes burning with frustrated rage.

The Rio Kid did not believe that he had exposed himself in the fight to save the Texans. It had been night, and Kinny was dead, as was Spiky Sam. The gang, after the abortive fight, had split up, every man running to save himself. But he was ready to draw and fight it out if need be.

Lowndes saw him in the mirror as the Rio Kid pushed close. Brick turned, scowling.

"Hullo, Burns," he said. "So yuh made it. Nasty mess. Somebody crossed us. Them lobos got on to us and were ready. Yuh get hurt?"

A bullet had cut a chunk of felt from Pryor's Stetson, and he indicated it.

"Clipped my hair, and I took some scratches, but I was lucky, Boss. Me'n Kinny tried to work over to help Spiky Sam but they got Kinny in the first volley. It was a lot harder'n it looked. There must have been dozens of 'em around, layin' for us."

Aloysius, the gambler, watched the speaker. But the Rio Kid could detect nothing in the manner of either man to indicate that they suspected him. There was no reason to, since he had managed to cover himself in the fight. Lowndes reached in his pocket and brought out a ten-dollar bill.

"Here's yore pay, Burns," he said. "Stick around, though. We don't always get the worst of it. I'll have more work for yuh pronto. It ain't our way to stay licked. We'll go after them clodhoppers and show 'em what for."

Brick turned back to his drink with a short nod. The Rio Kid, in his guise of an outlaw, a lowly member of the gang, was dismissed.

He left the saloon, but waited in the shadows at the side of the place. A carriage drew up after a time and a gentleman clad in the height of fashion stepped out and handed down a silken-gowned young woman with yellow hair and rouged cheeks. The man was George Hansinger, returning from a short trip.

Hansinger went into the Rollins House. The

young woman left him in the lobby, and the Rio Kid, through an open window, saw Lowndes and Aloysius signal the bearded chief. Hansinger nodded, and walked to the staircase at the back of the lobby.

"They were waitin' for him, no doubt of that," thought Pryor.

He wanted to check up, get all possible information for Dodge. Hansinger seemed to top Lowndes and Aloysius. He might be the king-pin of all Cheyenne's underworld, the Rio Kid was thinking as the two lieutenants followed Hansinger up the stairs to the second floor of the hotel.

The Rio Kid hurried to a side door and reached a flight of back steps by a short hall. On the second floor he heard voices, and made the right-angle turn in the corridor in time to see and hear the door close. Hansinger lived in the best rooms in the place.

The hall was empty at the moment. The Rio Kid moved toward the door, his feet making no sound on the thick green carpet runner on the floor. Wall-bracket lamps burned here and there, and he paused just outside Hansinger's door. He coud hear the talk through the thin panels, which had warped slightly, being made of green wood. The front stairs were only a few steps away, and he had to keep an eye on them and also listen in case somebody opened a door to emerge from another room.

GLASSES were tinkling inside Hansinger's room. Lowndes' harsh voice was audible as he reported:

"Boss, we got a lickin'! Them Texas fools was all ready, like they'd been tipped off. Spiky Sam and at least three, mebbe more men, got killed in the fight. We put up a grand scrap but they had the advantage of position. They winged me with a slug, and we split up and headed home."

Hansinger's voice was cool as he replied.

"Are yuh slippin', Brick? Yuh had personal charge of the job, didn't yuh?"

"Yeah," Brick said humbly. "I wouldn't even bother yuh, only guess who's out there with them Texans? Frank Warren, Tate's assistant! Seen him with my own eyes."

Hansinger's tones lost their coolness. He swore, and he was excited at Lowndes' news.

"I thought he must be dead! We hit him, didn't we? I figgered he'd fallen off his hoss in the chaparral and was buzzard-bait! Why hasn't he come back to Cheyenne, if he's alive?"

Lowndes, who hadn't liked the reprimand, was enjoying the effect of his startling news on Hansinger, the chief.

"From what we could see, Boss," he said, "Warren is wounded, bad hurt. They was nursin' him like a baby."

"I see. That may explain why he hasn't brought the roof down. Well, one thing's shore. We've got to dispose of him before he tells the

111

whole business. Cheyenne's not easy to hold and there's more and more competition. The one way to keep our pie is to jump fast and hard on any opposition, before it can build up. I've told yuh that often enough."

"Shall I get the boys ready, then?" asked Lowndes.

"Every possible man yuh can! I'll go along with yuh. We'll start tomorrow night. There won't be any slip-up this time!"

The Rio Kid saw a Stetson top appear between the banisters of the stairs and he had to hurry up the hall to the turn. He watched, in the shadow cast by the bulge of the wall, waiting for the man to enter a room. He thought the fellow was a hotel guest.

The man stopped. The Rio Kid, peeking around the corner, was startled plenty then, for he recognized the fellow's face, lit by a wall lamp near Hansinger's door.

"Drew Young!" he thought. "What's he doin' here?"

He was astounded. The tall, black-haired Texan wore leather pants and vest, and a great hat. He had on a pair of walnut-stocked six-shooters, and his face was scowling, set. His silver spurs caught the lamp-light as he knocked hard on Hansinger's door.

"Now what!" thought Pryor.

How had Young chanced to hunt up George Hansinger, Boss of Cheyenne? Then he remembered that the Texans had heard of Hansinger, that he himself had told them Hansinger was a power in the outlaw forces in the town!

Hansinger himself opened the door.

"What yuh want, sir?" the Rio Kid heard him challenge. "Are yuh shore yuh have the right room?"

"If this 'un belongs to George Hansinger, I have," replied Drew Young boldly.

"It might. Who are you, and what is it? I'm mighty busy this evenin'."

"When yuh hear what I got to say, yuh'll change yore tune," boasted the visitor. "My handle's Drew Young and I'm from old Gus Jennings' cow camp. I savvy who you are. We got a loco young fool out there named Frank Warren who keeps babblin' yore name—Hansinger. And an hombre called the Rio Kid is sneakin' on yore trail."

Hansinger opened the door wide, and Drew Young, the traitor, stepped in. The door closed.

The angry Rio Kid had a hand gripping his Colt butt. The black-haired Texan, Drew Young, had doublecrossed his friends! He had come to sell out to Hansinger and throw in his lot with the outlaws of Cheyenne. There would be profit in it for Young, and sweet revenge.

He would make sure that Warren and the Rio Kid were killed.

"That egg was rottener'n I figgered, even!" thought the Rio Kid, getting a rein on his temper.

He moved toward Hansinger's door again,

113

and he could hear Drew Young telling everything:

"—Rio Kid sidewinder worked in with yore gang, posed as one of yuh. He slugged a feller named Kinny and give Jennings the alarm so's the ranchers was all ready."

"Why, that Dave Burns was with Kinny!" gasped Brick Lowndes. "He must be the Rio Kid! By hook, I never suspected the skunk!"

"Harry Mackintosh vouched for Burns to us," said Aloysius.

"Mackintosh is all right," said Lowndes. "Somehow this Rio Kid tricked Mac into giving him an introduction, otherwise I'd never have trusted him till he'd been tested out."

"This Rio Kid," continued Drew Young, proud of the effect his information was having on these powerful people, "is spyin' for General Dodge and the railroad. I heard Gus Jennings say so. Dodge means to smash yuh. I come to you because I'm sick of them fools back there. I reckon yuh'll treat me right, gents. All I want is a fair share."

"Yuh're in, son," promised Hansinger. His voice was hoarse with rage. "Everything yuh say checks. Now, Brick, the first thing we must do is catch this Rio Kid traitor and sink him. Next, we'll wipe out Warren and Jennings, then we'll see about Dodge. If a drygulcher's slug'll do the trick, I'll find the right man to finish Dodge's career! Someone I can deal with will finish the railroad."

"I'm goin' out and find that Rio Kid right now!" cried Brick Lowndes. "In a jiffy every man we got in Cheyenne'll be gunnin' for him."

THE RIO KID hurried to the corner just as Lowndes burst from the door of Hansinger's suite. It was time to leave. What the redhead said was true—there would be a hundred guns hunting him within minutes.

He went down the rear stairs, and as he made for the side exit, Brick Lowndes glimpsed him through the hall. Immediately Lowndes let out a shout. He whipped a Colt and fired, but the Rio Kid heard the sharp sound as the bullet drove into the wooden panels, and then he had jumped outside.

Lowndes had aides around the hotel, who answered his calls. Gunmen and gamblers took up the chase after the hurrying Rio Kid. Saber was in a corral a block up the street from the Rollins House. The retreating Rio Kid, knowing he would be trapped and killed without mercy in Cheyenne, now they were aware of his identity, ran with desperate speed along the rutted lane which lay behind the buildings of the main line.

He knew that Brick Lowndes was hunting him, warning all the killers in town to shoot him on sight. He could hear men calling to one another. Lowndes had seen him turn, perhaps had guessed his moves, for as he passed a lane leading to Main Street he saw two armed men coming toward him. They yelled, started running at him, then he was past the turn and kept going.

Gunshots rapped in the night. The Rio Kid made the corral, and snatched his saddle from the peg at the back of the stable. He whistled, "Said the Big Black Charger to the Little White Mare," strains of an old Army tune, which brought the dun galloping to him. Slapping on his rig, he cinched up, and was mounting, swinging Saber along the lane to leave Cheyenne, when a whistling bullet passed his ear.

He drew a Colt, firing at flashes of enemy guns. They were coming at him, and he started the dun off, hoping to break through before they could concentrate on him.

He made the next turn, and decided to take it, to shut them off from firing at him. As he jerked his reins, a dark figure jumped from his right, and fired on him. Only the veering of his horse saved him. He sent a hasty slug at the attacker, who uttered a screech and sank to his knees in the dirt.

"Lowndes is throwin' a cordon around the block!" the hunted man thought.

The Rio Kid hugged the swift dun, keeping low, as Saber picked up speed. The *clop-clop* of hoofs rang as they hit cobbles up the way. Riders and running men were trying to head him off.

The Rio Kid blasted his way out of Cheyenne, the wild town!

CHAPTER XII
General Dodge Cleans Up

IT WAS near midnight when the Rio Kid sighted the lantern lights of Rail's End. There were guards around the camp, the tents and portable shacks, and the great piles of supplies that had been dumped on the prairie. The hard-working crews slept, but guards had to be on watch for Indians in the night, and valuable equipment had to be protected from both white and red marauders.

A sentry challenged Bob Pryor, and he slowed to make himself known. Murphy, one of the special railroad police, the man who had stopped him, knew the Rio Kid and greeted him heartily as he recognized the horseman.

"Is General Dodge here?" asked Pryor.

"Shore is," Murphy answered. "He's sleepin' in his car over there, Rio Kid."

"I got to see him pronto."

"Kelly's guardin' over there. Speak to him."

Grenville Dodge had been enjoying a brief nap. The chief engineer of the new transcontinental railroad seldom had time to rest for long periods. But he was alert, judging the situation as the Rio Kid quickly told him all he had learned in Cheyenne. Dodge's thick mustache worked and his deep-set eyes flashed.

"Speed," he declared. "That's what we need, Rio Kid. You've done a fine job in Cheyenne. Now I'll strike and strike hard, before Hansinger gets set."

Dodge rang a hand bell on his table, and Kelly, the big Irish special policeman who had charge of Dodge's railroad officers came to the car door.

"Rout out the boys, Kelly," Dodge ordered. "I want every man who's in camp and who can be spared. We're going to clean up Cheyenne."

"Phew!" Kelly whistled, then grinned widely. "That'll be a jog, Gin'ral! But we'll be ready to start in half an hour."

Dodge was pulling on his boots. He had been sleeping in his clothing.

"Have a drink," he told Pryor.

"Did my friend Celestino Mireles reach yuh last evenin', General?" asked the Rio Kid, as he poured the drink.

"Oh, yes. I had your report, and I sent a surgeon off at once, as you requested, to care for that wounded man in the cow camp."

Dodge always acted promptly. He had had long military experience, had been a splendid officer during the Civil War. Now he used the discipline he had learned in running his hordes of workers and he marshalled his fighters in the same manner.

"I don't know all the thieves in Cheyenne, General," said the Rio Kid, as they left the car which was Dodge's home. "But I shore can point out Hansinger and his two chief aides, Lowndes and Aloysius. Then I savvy thirty or forty more of the rank and file who went on a night attack after Jennings' cows, as well as a few more I've seen around town."

"We'll arrest this Hansinger and his cronies," declared Dodge, "and throw a scare into the ones we don't nab. With the boss out of the way, things should quiet down for a time, anyway."

"Sooner or later the decent folks will take over, General," the Rio Kid said, in a tone of certainty.

"That's right," Dodge agreed. "Frontier conditions can't last forever."

Dodge's chief purpose, when he had sent the Rio Kid to spy out Cheyenne, had been to insure the safety of the workers when they were in the town. He had had no special civic purpose in mind, for he was fully occupied with the enormous detail of his job, of running a railroad across the vast wild continent, something never before attempted, and said by some to be impossible.

The Central Pacific and the Dodge line were racing, each trying to gain the lands and bonus offered by the Government for every mile built. Everything Dodge did was directed toward the accomplishment of this end. But since the railroad meant to build shops in Cheyenne, and there had been troubles with lot-jumpers there, cleaning up Cheyenne was in line with his business.

As they were making ready to ride, Celestino Mireles came up. After the young Mexican had delivered the Rio Kid's report to Dodge, he had been resting at the camp. Buffalo Bill Cody was with him, and the chief of buffalo hunters shook hands heartily with the Rio Kid.

"I ran into camp for the evenin', to pick up supplies and ammunition, Rio Kid," said Cody. "Glad I did. It gives me a chance to join the fun in this Cheyenne business."

Dodge kept the Rio Kid at his side, with Kelly on the other hand, as he led the heavily armed band of special police toward the settlement. Some of them, such as Giles Kelly, were deputy Federal marshals, empowered to make arrests in any state or territory of the United States. En route, riding under the powdered sky, and with a chunk of yellow moon giving sufficient light, Dodge talked further with Bob Pryor, learning all the details concerning Hansinger and the wild bunch in Cheyenne.

THE GENERAL was particularly interested in the story of Frank Warren.

"I was acquainted with Paul Tate, the editor of the *Times*," he said. "He was a fine man. Perhaps this young fellow Warren will be able to tell us just what happened to Tate, if the doctor can cure him."

"That's what I figured, General," said the Rio Kid. "The way Hansinger and Lowndes acted, Warren's mighty dangerous to 'em."

Dodge was also intrigued by the account of Kinny's strange death.

"Natural gas!" he exclaimed. "I wonder how extensive it is."

"Don't know, sir," the Rio Kid told him. "Take an experienced engineer to find out, I s'pose."

"It would. I have a man, Halpers, who knows a great deal about gas and rock oil—petroleum."

"Mebbe he'll ride out some time with me, and check up. The stuff's a nuisance to ranchers. Likely to kill their cattle and ruin grass if it leaks out."

The first streak of the new dawn showed gray-white behind Dodge's forces as the cavalcade sighted Cheyenne.

"You lead the way, Rio Kid," ordered Dodge. "We'll go after Hansinger and Lowndes first, then try to sweep up the rank and file."

"We better hustle," Pryor advised. "We need to come in fast, before we show up on the skyline. They won't reckon on us hittin' so soon, if they're figgerin' on it at all."

Dodge and the Rio Kid stayed together, with half the police. Buffalo Bill Cody and Kelly had charge of the other half, and Mireles went with them to point out the quarters of Brick Lowndes and Aloysius, who dwelt in the Elite, across the main street from the Rollins, where Hansinger had his rooms.

The settlement was quieting down, in the fag end of the night. It was about four A.M., as the Rio Kid, General Grenville Dodge, Buffalo Bill, Kelly and the rest rushed through to the center of town. The Rio Kid threw a ring of armed men around the Rollins and, followed by Dodge, ran into the main bar.

Customers were still drinking at the bar, and others were at the gambling tables. Tired dance hall girls sat around, waiting for quitting time. Bartenders were cleaning up the mess after the night's fun.

According to the startled night clerk whom Dodge questioned, George Hansinger had gone up to his rooms a half hour before. The Rio Kid, with Dodge at his heels, ran upstairs. Pryor tried Hansinger's door but it was bolted, so he knocked softly.

After a time, Hansinger answered. "Who's that?"

"It's Brick, Chief," replied the Rio Kid, giving as good an imitation as he could of

Lowndes' voice. "I forgot somethin' mighty important."

Bare footsteps padded on the mat, and there was a squeak as the bolt was withdrawn. Hansinger was grumbling as he opened the door.

"I just turned in, Brick. What's so important—"

He broke off. A gunshot, two more, rapped sharply across the way, and men began shouting wildly. Hansinger was staring into the face of the Rio Kid, and he recognized Dodge, too.

"What's the meanin' of this?" he demanded indignantly.

The Rio Kid laughed as he kicked the door all the way open, and jumped inside. He wanted to be sure there were no gunnies in there.

Hansinger had on a mauve-colored nightshirt. His feet were bare, but his mustache was waxed. He looked ludicrous, and entirely harmless. The Rio Kid, from the side, patted him over quickly.

"Got anything under them duds?" he asked. "Say, yore costume's beautiful!"

Dodge and the men with him were grinning at Hansinger's discomfiture.

"I'm not armed," growled Hansinger, folding his arms and glaring. It was all he could do. If he had a weapon in the room, it wasn't near enough for him to get at it.

"May I ask the meanin' of this outrageous intrusion, General Dodge?" snorted Hansinger.

"Off your horse, Hansinger," snapped Dodge. "You're under arrest."

"On what charges, sir?"

"As chief of the deviltry in Cheyenne."

"I demand my attorney be called."

Dodge gave an impatient exclamation. He seized Hansinger by the shoulder, jerked him around and threw him at Murphy, the powerful marshal. Murphy gripped him.

"Handcuff him, Murph," ordered Dodge, "take him over to the jug and see he's locked up."

With Hansinger captured, the Rio Kid was aware of the increasing hubbub across the way. He ran to a front window, and stepped onto a narrow balcony from which he could see the street below and the corner where the Elite stood. Men were spilling out of doors and windows, some with guns going, others just trying to reach safety.

LIGHT had come up enough so that he could recognize some of them. Brick Lowndes suddenly appeared, hurtling from the side door, with two Colts working. The redhead had on pants and shirt, but he had run out without his boots and hat. He made a tentative turn toward the rear of the Elite, perhaps to get his horse. But Buffalo Bill Cody and Mireles, with some of the Dodge fighters, rounded the turn, guns blaring.

Lowndes saw two of his men go down—

tough rustlers who had made the run over to Jennings' cow camp. Brick swung, darting to the corner of the building, followed by those of his friends who could make it. They paused to make a stand at the corner, as the Rio Kid, meaning to get in the scrap, went over the balcony rail and slid down a waterpipe to the sidewalk.

Lowndes and his men held the corner. Buffalo Bill, Celestino, and Dodge's police were trying to work up the side street and drive them out. Chunks of brick and splinters of wood filled the air as big slugs struck. The Rio Kid, taking advantage of the din, was half-way across the street before Brick happened to look over his shoulder and saw him coming.

"Throw down, Brick!" shouted Pryor, his voice carrying above the battle. "Yuh're under arrest!"

Lowndes' vicious face twisted with his rage as he whipped his Colts around on the Rio Kid and let go. The Rio Kid, dropping to his knee in the middle of the street, took a second-fraction for better aim. Lowndes got in the first shot but it whistled past Pryor's ear, and then the Rio Kid raised his thumb off his hammer.

He knew he had hit. Lowndes got off another one but it was low, driving into the dirt road. The redheaded man staggered, putting out a hand to steady himself against the brick wall of the Elite. The Rio Kid shot again, and blasted the bunch at the corner. Hastily they split up, running every which way.

Buffalo Bill Cody and Mireles came charging around the turn as the firing eased off.

When the Rio Kid reached Brick Lowndes, Hansinger's lieutenant was on the ground, lying crumpled on his guns. One of Pryor's bullets had hit his chest, another had ranged into his heart, and he was done.

The Rio Kid joined his own companions and they hurried through the streets, picking up men whom Pryor and Mireles knew were members of the outlaw gangs which had ruled the settlement. The Rio Kid caught Harry Mackintosh and his outlaw partner Jim, at their shack. He watched for Drew Young, the traitor from Jennings' party, but never saw the Texan in town.

"We caught that Aloysius scoundrel right off," said Buffalo Bill, as they paused for a breath. "He let out a screech like a woman, and that's what warned that Brick hombre. I believe yuh can scare a lot of information out of Aloysius. He ain't got much fight in him, Rio Kid."

The Rio Kid nodded, but had no time for Aloysius right then. For he and General Dodge raged through Cheyenne that cool dawn, cleaning up the wild town.

CHAPTER XIII
New Life

YOUNG Frank Warren's consciousness returned in a confused roaring. A bearded man stood over him, holding his wrist, taking his pulse.

"Oh, my head—my head!" Warren muttered, trying to touch his splitting brow. There was a wadded bandage there, however.

"You'll be all right son. Take it easy." The voice of the elderly man who spoke to him was kindly, his touch gentle.

Behind the bearded man stood several people. One was a beautiful girl with thick, fair hair. There was anxiety in her long-lashed blue eyes as she watched Warren. For a moment he forgot the ache in his head, and he felt shy, yet there was a fascination which kept his eyes riveted to hers.

He was hardly aware of the rest of them—

a middle-aged woman with a kindly face who looked something like the younger, a huge man with a red face and seamed, smiling eyes, and others.

The girl stepped forward. Warren knew he had never seen her before, but he felt a strange emotion, as though he knew her. Especially when she spoke, and smiled at him.

"How do you feel, Frank?" she asked. "Are you very sick?"

"No—I guess I'm all right."

He sought to remember, but could not. She knew him, addressing him by name. It was annoying not to be able to call her name, not even to guess who she was. He was certain that if he had ever seen her he could never have forgotten her. She was the prettiest girl he had ever looked upon and he felt drawn to her by powerful magnetism.

"Where am I?" he asked. "In Cheyenne? Is it morning already?"

"No. You're a long way from Cheyenne, Frank." The girl took his hand. "Would you like a drink of water?"

"Yes, I would."

His surroundings were clearer now. He could see that he was lying on a blanket bed, beneath a spread canvas which kept the sun off him. The bearded man seemed to be a doctor.

"Is—is Hansinger here?" Warren asked weakly. "Tate—he died. Did Johnny Three Snakes get me out—or what?"

The big man with the red face stepped forward and knelt beside him.

"Reckon yuh need to be brought up to date, my boy. Yuh took a slug in the head which shut off yore mind for a while. It's many days since yuh was wounded. My handle is Gus Jennings, and we're all from Texas, come to Wyomin' with our herds to settle. Except this gent—he's Doc Robson, sent out by General Dodge and the Rio Kid to extract the bullet from yore skull.

"That Crow Injun brought yuh safe out of Cheyenne, and the Rio Kid picked yuh up on the prairie, then turned yuh over to us. This Hansinger scoundrel yuh mention'll be arrested before too long. Tate, yore friend, was killed, and yore newspaper burnt up. This here is my daughter Alyse. She's nursed yuh steady since yuh come to us."

"Perhaps that's why I'm so sure I know you," said Warren, in a troubled voice. "It's—hard to remember."

She looked a bit hurt for a moment, as though an old friend had snubbed her. But then she smiled, and the touch of her hand was warm, comforting as she skillfully helped him drink from a tin cup she had brought.

"She's been nursin' yuh like a baby, son," said Jennings.

"He'll be all right now. He's got a strong heart and the worst is over." Dr. Robson spoke to Jennings. "Keep him down and quiet for a day or two, and he can eat anything he wants after this morning. Your daughter and Mrs. Jennings know how to change the dressings. If anything seems wrong, you can send for me again, but I'm sure he'll be fine."

The surgeon had to return to Dodge's camp. There were always accidents, men to be taken care of there. Warren was out of danger, and with the bullet extracted from his skull he should recover rapidly, with his youth and natural strength to help.

Warren stayed on his blanket bed, under the canopy, and after a few hours began to feel much better. Alyse Jennings was at hand, ready to give him a drink. She brought him warm beef broth and he drank it slowly, watching her, trying to draw out the details of his long illness, to fill in that blank space in his brain.

She seemed to know all about him and his experiences. She kept mentioning somebody called "the Rio Kid," and Gus Jennings had talked about that person, too.

"Who is this Rio Kid?" inquired Warren at last.

Alyse smiled. "That's so. I keep forgetting you—you were too sick to know anybody all that time. Well, the Rio Kid's name is Bob Pryor. He's very good-looking and a marvelous rider and scout. If it hadn't been for him, my father and many of our friends would have been killed—and so would you. The Rio Kid brought you to us, you know. You should be very grateful to him, just as we all are."

WARREN felt a twinge in his heart which he recognized as jealousy, envy. He concluded that Alyse must be in love with this famous, debonair scout, the Rio Kid. But he was quickly ashamed of this base emotion. He told himself he had no right to demand anything further from these people who had already done so much for him. There was a silence. Warren found he was clenching his fists.

"The Rio Kid's evidently a fine fellow," he said, his voice low. He managed to ask: "I— I suppose he's your fiancé, Alyse?"

When she smiled, his whole being responded with the greatest joy. He had never seen anyone who swayed him so. There had been girls in his life, but they had been no more than passing fancies, girls he had admired. He was drawn to Alyse by irresistible powers. Cold sweat prickled on him. It seemed to him she would never answer his question, but at last she said:

"Why, no, I'm not engaged to the Rio Kid, Frank. I do like him a lot, though. Any girl would admire such a man."

"You—you're not spoken for, then?" he asked huskily.

"Not yet—not by anyone I'd have."

Her eyes met his. They were frank, open, innocent. He felt an upsurge of joy. If she was not engaged, then he might have a chance. But he felt humble. She was too beautiful, too wonderful to hope for.

"The Rio Kid and General Dodge are going after Hansinger and his gangs in Cheyenne right now," continued Alyse, sitting down by him. "So I don't think we'll need to worry about our enemies any more, Frank. They came here to steal our cattle herd, but the Rio Kid stopped them and we drove them away. It was a terrible battle, in the darkness. One of our boys died and several were wounded, but they lost four and a lot were hit. It was then they discovered you were in our camp, and the Rio Kid told us that Hansinger wanted you killed more than anything."

Warren nodded. The mention of George Hansinger brought it all back, clearly. He shuddered.

"Hansinger's a terrible man, Alyse. Boss of Cheyenne, responsible for a lot of killings and robberies and skullduggery. I—I saw him kill my boss, Paul Tate, editor of the *Times*. He shot him down in cold blood, because Tate meant to run a story telling what a scoundrel Hansinger is."

Alyse was much interested as Warren described the deadly scene at the newspaper office. His own memory failed him, after he had leaped on the nearest horse in the back street. His mind was a blank from that instant until he had returned to a new life in the cow camp. But she could fill in the spaces.

"A Crow Indian named Johnny Three Snakes brought you out of Cheyenne, Frank," she told him. "My father told you that."

"Johnny Three Snakes!" Now Warren was remembering anew. He had cast his bread upon the waters, when he had befriended the Indian, and it had certainly returned with interest. "Yes, I remember Johnny was around that evening. He must have been nearby and heard the ruckus. And he helped me out."

"Then the Rio Kid picked you up and he brought you here," Alyse repeated.

The gaps were being filled in by the repetition, but he knew that Alyse had not told him of the long hours and days she had spent, nursing him. That had been mentioned by her father, Gus Jennings. He had been entirely helpless, without doubt.

"You've done a lot for me, too, Alyse," he said humbly. "I'm mighty thankful to you. I know how hard you've worked, looking out for me." He could not take his eyes from hers.

"I was happy doing it, Frank! But you mustn't talk too much. You're not strong, you know. Try to take a nap."

She was insistent that he rest. He closed his eyes and drifted into a sound sleep.

When he awoke, it was dark, and Alyse was watching over him. She brought him a meal of stewed meat and bread. He found his appetite good, and when he opened his eyes the next morning, Warren felt like a different man. Strength flowed in him, and the will to move.

Alyse let him sit up that day, but she would not allow him to move around much. His legs were shaky, but he was on the way to recovery.

JUST before sunset, the second day after the bullet had been removed, the ranchers had come back to camp for the night, and were having their evening meal, when a large young man rode into the circle. He dismounted, and came to Gus Jennings.

"Well?" said Jennings harshly. "What yuh want, Drew?"

"Gus, I come back to apologize," Drew Young said contritely. "I acted like a fool and I admit it. Will yuh shake and let me come back? I'll do better from now on."

Drew Young spoke with a beaten dog's air. All the arrogance was gone from his bearing as he begged for forgiveness. He squatted beside Jennings, speaking so that they could all hear him.

"I rode out and camped by myself in the mountains. I thought it all over and I seen the light. I had to come back, if only to tell yuh I'm sorry."

Gus Jennings cleared his throat. He exchanged glances with his cronies.

"Oh, let the boy come back, Gus," said Sara

Jennings. "Here, Drew, sit down and have a bite. You look peaked."

They were good-hearted, quick to let bygones be bygones. Frank Warren sat among them, beside Alyse. He did not know Drew Young from Adam, for the hot-headed man had come into his life while he was suffering from the amnesia brought on by the bullet in his skull.

Young came to him, and held out his hand in an open, manly way.

"Howdy, Warren. I want to ask yore pardon for the way I acted—and yores, too, Alyse."

Warren smiled and shook hands. "You have the advantage of me, sir," he said. "I take it we've met before, but I haven't been able to remember anything since the time I left Cheyenne, many days ago. But you have any pardon necessary from me."

Young's black eyes narrowed a bit, but he grinned as he pumped Warren's arm.

"Yuh're all right, Warren, even if yuh ain't from Texas. I hope we can be friends. I'm mighty happy to be back, folks. I savvy what a jackass I acted like."

His apology was so handsome, so open, that soon they were belittling what he had done to deserve the punishment meted out by Jennings. Jennings had beaten him up, and confined him. Then Young had run off, during the night.

Drew Young willingly helped clean up the camp. He begged to be allowed to do any kind of work. He laid out his bedrole and then volunteered for guard duty, for Jennings insisted on keeping sentries out to watch the camp and herd, as he had been advised to do by the Rio Kid.

CHAPTER XIV
Plans

WITH no alarm being sounded, the night passed and day broke. Frank Warren slept well, and in the morning he felt entirely normal. He dressed, walked around some, and ate a big breakfast.

The cowmen had a great deal of work to do. They were getting ready for it when the go-ahead signal came from the Rio Kid that Hansinger was no longer a menace, and they could build their new homes in the wonderful grazing country of southeast Wyoming. Timber had to be marked for cutting, pens got ready. There were a thousand things to think about, and besides the herds had to be guarded and cared for.

Gus Jennings and his friends left immediately after breakfast. A few remained in camp as guards, though all were of the opinion that by now the Rio Kid and General Dodge would have dealt Hansinger a death blow. Drew Young, who had been on sentry duty through the small hours, stayed in his blanket roll, sleeping.

The sun came up, yellow and warm. Frank Warren walked around the camp some more, and helped Alyse and her mother. For there were many tasks, cleaning up, mending, washing, getting ready to feed the voracious Texans.

It was hot when the sun reached the noon peak, and Drew Young aroused, stretched, pulled on his boots, and hat, and buckled on his gun-belts. Young winked at Warren as he came to get some coffee and a bite.

"A-ah, had a good sleep," he said, in a friendly way. "How you feelin' today, buck?"

"I'm fine, thanks."

In spite of Young's apparent heartiness, Warren did not like Drew too much, as he grew acquainted. There was a sense of harshness, which the Texan sought to hide. Once he caught Young watching him, over the rim of his tin cup as he drank coffee, and Warren was sure there was malevolence in the man's eyes.

He kept away from Young, but soon the Texan saddled his powerful, dark-hided mustang, placed his carbine in the boot, and made ready to ride. Drew went off to the northwest, as though he intended to join one of the working parties and lend a hand.

Alyse and her mother dressed Frank Warren's head wound after lunch. It was healing well, they said. At their insistence, Warren lay down for a nap but he was slept out. He watched Alyse as she worked.

It was nearly three o'clock that afternoon when a sentry on the east sang out to others closer to the camp. The word was passed along, and quickly those around the wagons grew alert. Warren got up. He was nervous about the approach of riders, as the guards reported, but soon it was announced that there were only three, and that one was the Rio Kid, their friend.

"I'll be glad to meet him and thank him myself," Warren told Alyse.

A fine-looking young man rode in on a mouse-colored dun, which had a black stripe down his spine—"the breed that never dies." He wore an Army Stetson, and Army pistols, black cavalry boots, a blue tunic and whipcord breeches. Vitality was written in the lithe, sure figure, in the strong face. With him was a lean young Mexican, in the form-fitted clothing and big sombrero such men affected on the frontier. And there was an older man, in engineer's clothing and boots, on a white mare.

The Rio Kid was welcomed with open arms. Mrs. Jennings kissed him, and made him sit down as she brought out food and drink. Alyse brought Warren to him.

"This is Frank, Rio Kid! He's all right. Isn't it wonderful?"

She was very happy. The Rio Kid smiled and shook hands. He appraised Warren with a keen blue eye and nodded.

"Glad to see yuh so chipper, Warren. Yuh had a tough time of it."

"I have a great deal to thank you for, Rio Kid."

Warren sat near Pryor, and told him of his gratitude, but the Rio Kid waved it aside.

"Yeah, we took care of Hansinger," said the Rio Kid, in answer to the questions they fired at him. "Hansinger is in Cheyenne jail, with a bunch of his men, Aloysius among 'em. Dodge and a bunch of us hit 'em the other night. We shot Brick Lowndes dead."

"Lowndes dead!" cried Warren. "I believe he's the one who wounded me. I recall that Aloysius and Brick were firing at me as I tried to escape."

"Brick won't shoot at yuh any more, my boy. A lot of 'em run for it, and Cheyenne's clean, for a while, anyways."

The engineer with the Rio Kid and Mireles was Cass Halpers, one of Dodge's assistants.

"I figgered Halpers would savvy about that natural gas," explained the Rio Kid. "I had to make a run back to the railroad camp to pick him up, and he was out, workin', so it took a while."

"NATURAL gas?" repeated Warren. He remembered something in which Tate had been interested, a feature they had printed in the newspaper.

"Is there gas around here?" he asked.

"Looks like it. Halpers can say whether it's extensive or not."

"That's interesting," said Warren. "Paul Tate talked about it a lot, and about lighting Cheyenne's streets with natural gas. It hasn't been done before, you know, in this country."

"Gas lights?" Mrs. Jennings was amazed. "Land sakes, what will they thing up next! Why, it would blow up and explode everything, wouldn't it?"

Halpers spoke. "No, ma'am. Not with the proper burner. It's a great thing. The men who run Cheyenne have been talking it over. If you have enough gas here, it's the nearest spot to the city. It could be piped in easy enough."

The Rio Kid was heartily eating the good food which had been set before him. Mrs. Jennings and Alyse kept urging him and his companions to take more.

"By the way, Rio Kid," Alyse said, "Drew Young came back. He's so sorry about it all. And I'm sure he'll apologize to you when he gets in this evening."

The Rio Kid choked on a mouthful of beef stew and bread. His face went purple and he jumped to his feet.

"Huh! What's that? Yuh say Drew Young's been here?"

The Rio Kid was startled as he heard that the black-haired Texan had dared return to the cow camp.

"Why, cuss him! I hunted all over Cheyenne for him. I figger he'd took the road for shore!"

"Cheyenne?" asked Alyse. "Was he in Cheyenne?"

"Was he! He hooked up with Hansinger and near give away our whole play. He's the dirtiest doublecrosser I ever hope to meet. If I ever get him in my gunsights, he won't—" He broke off, with a shrug. "Now tell me how he come to show his ugly face here, folks."

They described how Drew Young had returned, crawling, begging forgiveness.

"Cuss him!" the Rio Kid raged. "Why'd he do it? 'Course he didn't savvy I knew he had turned yuh all over to Hansinger. He spilt the beans about Dodge and me, and told Hansinger he'd help him finish you people off. The only reason he'd come back here would be to get even some way."

The Rio Kid was thinking, thinking hard. He knew that Young was a bad one, rotten all the way through.

"Which way'd he go?" he asked, at last. "I'll ride out and see if I can pick him up."

He left the camp with Mireles. They rode in the direction which Young had taken, but after an hour they sighted Gus Jennings with several of his friends, and turned down to greet them. Jennings was furiously angry when he learned about Drew Young's perfidy. He agreed with the Rio Kid.

"Yeah, he's come back, mebbe to get even with us, Rio Kid. When he comes in this evenin', I'll grab him and we'll tie him up and turn him over to the law in Cheyenne."

It was five P.M. when they got back to the camp. The sun was lowering in the sky, reddening a bit, although the day was long as it always was in summer. Drew Young was not at the camp, but the Rio Kid saw Buffalo Bill Cody who had come in a few minutes before on Brigham, his well-known mustang.

"Howdy, Rio Kid—got news." Cody's handsome face was grave as he greeted Pryor. "Hansinger's out!"

The Rio Kid swore. "How'd he do it? Escape?"

"No. Dodge had a call, had to leave town, so Hansinger's lawyer woke up a magistrate they knew and he signed a writ. They had to let the sidewinder loose on bail. Figgered yuh ought to know Hansinger was on the prowl, so I hustled here on yore trail."

"He left Cheyenne?"

"Soon as he was free. Best I could do was to find out that he was seen headin' west out of the city."

"Wonder if Drew Young's comin' here is

connected with Hansinger?" mused the Rio Kid.

Frank Warren, and in a lesser degree, Gus Jennings and the ranchers, were dangerous witnesses against George Hansinger. Dodge had said so, when they had tossed Hansinger into Cheyenne jail, purple nightshirt and all. They needed reliable witnesses, especially Frank Warren, who had actually seen Hansinger kill a victim. Aloysius, in the lockup, had proved tougher than they had expected. He knew that Hansinger would do everything in his power to have his men freed.

"Plenty of Hansinger's bunch got away from us, too," the Rio Kid thought.

The Rio Kid was worried as he drew Cody aside.

"Bill," he said, "we got to work. I been hopin' this Drew Young skunk would appear, but mebbe he spied us and got suspicious. I have a feelin' he's come back here to pull somethin' for Hansinger, who's on the loose. Yuh s'pose we could trail Young?"

"We can try," said Cody.

Both Buffalo Bill and the Rio Kid were the most expert of scouts. The slightest sign told such men a whole story. The folks in camp could point out where Drew Young had saddled his black horse, and indentations had been retained by the soft earth along the stream bank. They familiarized themselves with the peculiarities of the shod hoofs of the mustang which Young had been riding. Nail marks, a little crack in one shoe, and a habit that black had of sliding his right rear hoof when he turned—these would all help.

"C'mon. We ain't got much time before dark, Bill."

The Rio Kid, Cody and Mireles left the camp, hoping to stay on the trail of Young's black mustang.

These men had stalked Indians, savages whose wild instincts made them as cunning and hard to trap as beasts, and whose brains made them much more dangerous. Cody rode on the right of the Rio Kid, a few yards away, covering that section. The Rio Kid watched the center, while Celestino was at his left. For a time they were able to pick up the sign without dismounting. It led in a northwesterly direction from the camp, skirting the herd bedding grounds, and passing the spot where Kinny had been gassed.

They went through the narrows, along which the defunct Spiky Sam had brought them in the approach on the Texans' herd. The Rio Kid had his bearings, and looked curiously about. The aspect was different from what it had been when he had come through in the dark.

They hit a faint cross trail. This was a path which had first been laid out by animals, wild creatures whose instincts led them the easiest route to the nearest water. The Indians had

145

followed the animals, and the white man had come along after the savages.

They spent ten minutes checking up before Cody picked out the telltale hoofs of the black mustang. It had turned to the west. There were other hoofprints, but they were two or three days older than Young's.

"Quite a bunch come through here—I'd say it was Tuesday last," remarked Buffalo Bill, and the Rio Kid agreed.

The way grew increasingly rough, with stones sticking up, and steep up-grades to be climbed. The light was fast dying. In the hills they could no longer see the sun itself, only the redness of the western sky. They had to move with some caution, for they did not want to run over Drew Young and into ambush.

Keeping on, they reached a local summit, and could look out on a wild expanse of rocks, woods, and a creek canyon cut through the ridges.

But they knew the jig was up for dark was at hand. The light was purple, the sky losing its gorgeous hues. Night caught them on the downgrade and they could no longer keep the trail without showing lights to check. It would be slow, too.

For an hour they tried lighting matches under a poncho, to check the signs, but they kept losing it. Young had turned off the faint Indian trail, and before them showed the black swale of the rocks and forests.

"We'll have to camp for the night, Bill," said the Rio Kid.

They unsaddled, and spread their blankets. There was a moon rising, and stars powdered the sky. The breeze was cool, and they wrapped blankets about them.

The Rio Kid sat up, staring at the dark wilderness. Suddenly he said:

"Look at that!"

Cody got up, Mireles too, and the three peered at the faint red glow.

" 'Tain't far away!" exclaimed Buffalo Bill. "It's over in that crik canyon there!"

"Cook fire, and for warmth, too!" declared the Rio Kid. "They got it hid in the rocks, but the glare reflects upwards!"

It was too good to miss, thought the Rio Kid. The chances were that a camp-fire in such a spot would have been made by the man they were seeking—by Drew Young and his companions. They silently saddled up and rode on down the slope.

Closer to the telltale fire glow, Buffalo Bill and the Rio Kid left their horses with Mireles and continued on foot, after removing their riding boots and substituting moccasins which made no sounds as did spurred leather. They rubbed dirt on their faces, to kill the shine of flesh, and made sure nothing metallic could clank as they moved.

With the stealth of stalking tigers, Cody and Pryor made the approach. Cody reached out after a while and touched the Rio Kid's arm. "Sentry," he breathed.

Against the sky they could make out the Stetson and upper body of a man on guard at the black mouth of the creek canyon, where the hills rose. In there was the fire which had led them to the spot.

CHAPTER XV
Lights for Cheyenne

QUICKLY the Rio Kid and Buffalo Bill Cody flattened to the ground, hardly breathing, as they heard footsteps. A second man approached from the inner canyon, and stopped by the sentry.

"Go ahead in, pard, and get some shut-eye," he mumbled. "I'll take over now."

The guard changed. Rifles gleamed in the faint light. The wind brought the drift of wood smoke from the fire that was hidden by a slanting rock wall. The narrow gate was the only way in that the two scouts could make out from where they lay and it was downwind. The Rio Kid touched Cody.

"I'm goin' in and get him, Bill," he breathed in the scout's ear. "Cover me."

He began the slow stalk, while Buffalo Bill watched every instant in case the guard should hear something and shoot at the sound. A little stone rolled, clacked softly against another. The sentry glanced that way but the Rio Kid was unmoving, and could not be seen among the boulders.

It took him twenty minutes to cover the few yards to the sentinel. Then he was so close he could hear the man's heavy breathing, could hear the fellow curse now and again, as he slapped at biting insects. The Rio Kid had to wait until he turned his back again. When the guard at last swung around the Rio Kid hit him from behind.

Cody slid up to join him.

"Stick here, Bill," the Rio Kid whispered. "I'm goin' in."

Voices could be heard from around the turn. The Rio Kid tiptoed closer. He paused, to peer around the jutting rock. The fire was popular that cool night. Men were huddled about it, some lying in blankets, others sitting up on flat rocks and consulting bottles of warming liquor. They had made the fire under a ledge, and believed it would be hidden, but the smooth face of a big rock had reflected enough light to the sky so that the Rio Kid's keen eyes had caught it.

Here, with the fire so close, he could see well. He counted about forty men in the camp. They had horses down the line, provisions and plenty of firearms. Among them he recognized several who had been on the night ride with

Spiky Sam and Brick Lowndes, and others he had seen around the Elite in Cheyenne.

George Hansinger and Drew Young sat on a fallen tree trunk, near the creek bank, talking together. They had their backs to the Rio Kid, and were between him and the main camp. A bottle of whisky passed between them.

Hansinger wore dark clothing, which was dirtied and torn in places. When he turned to speak to Young, the Rio Kid could see the man's spade beard and the glow of his eyes. To Pryor's left were some large boulders, chunks fallen from above. He began to inch toward these, to draw nearer Hansinger and the traitor Texan.

"Jig's about up in Cheyenne," Hansinger was saying. "I'm goin' to clean up and try Montana. I hear there's some sweet camps there."

"Yuh'll lose all that cash yuh put up for bail," said Young.

"No, I'll stand trial. We'll get rid of Warren. He's the only really dangerous witness. My lawyer says so. He can clear me with Warren out of the way. And I want to be around for a while, anyway."

The Rio Kid took it all in, pressed against the sharp shale.

"Dodge stands for law and order," philosophized Hansinger, tongue loosened by the liquor. "If it wasn't Dodge, though, it'd be someone else. These frontier towns last just so long. I have a lot of wealth in Cheyenne

151

I mean to liquidate. I'll fight Dodge in court till I have my money out."

"And the Rio Kid?"

"We'll take care of him, too. First, we'll see to Jennings, Warren and that bunch in the cow camp. It means a fortune—and I'm not the man to forget it's their fault that the Rio Kid came at me."

The Rio Kid listened, silent as one of the rocks he lay among. After a while, Hansinger, excited by the events of the past few days, and by what he contemplated for the morrow, ordered Young to turn in.

"Yuh need to be fresh, Drew," he said. "I expect yuh to go' in' and throw Jennings off guard. Yuh can shoot Warren at close range."

Pryor began his withdrawal. He reached Cody, and quickly told him what he had learned.

"They're goin' to hit the camp, and this time with no mistakes. Drew Young'll go in and distract 'em, so's Hansinger can rush the Texans. We want to make it fast. You go back to the hosses, tell Celestino to ride pronto and fetch Jennings and every fightin' man in camp!"

AS SOON as Bufflalo Bill was gone, the Rio Kid slipped back near the camp and crouched where Hansinger's sentry had been placed. He knew the relief had just been changed, and that, barring unforeseen accidents, he could count on several hours before the guard would again be replaced.

Once, an hour after Cody had hurried off, he heard someone approaching from the camp, and grew ready. A dark figure came within a few feet.

"All right, pard?" a man called softly.

"All right, pard," replied the Rio Kid hoarsely.

The time ran on. Each minute was precious. It was hard to wait, knowing that at any instant he might be discovered. But so far Hansinger's camp was quiet, only heavy snoring from the usual loud sleeper disturbing the peace.

Buffalo Bill came back, to make sure the Rio Kid was all right. They exchanged a few whispers, then Cody retired, to await the return of Mireles who had been sent to give the alarm.

The tense night passed. A telltale streak showed in the east. Soon the killers would be up, armed, ready to ride and destroy the Texans in their camp.

"Sst!"

It was Buffalo Bill hailing. The Rio Kid strained his eyes, and saw the scout's arm wave in the shadowy rocks. He moved out.

"Jennings is here, with all his men—Warren among 'em," Cody whispered. "What's yore orders?"

"Bring 'em in fast as yuh can, Bill, single file. We haven't much more time."

It was nearly four o'clock. The cool mist drifted from the waters of the purling creek, through the gap. Grayness occupied the world.

Pryor saw Buffalo Bill coming, his feet making no sounds. Behind him bulked a huge figure, Gus Jennings, carrying a rifle in his hands. There were more and more—Taylor, McNeill, Lytle, Bishop, Dagget, Jackson, and their sons. Frank Warren, too, had ridden with the party, insisting he be in the fight.

There was no time to spare. The Rio Kid clutched his carbine, full loaded his Colts were ready in their supple holsters. He led the way swiftly into the bivouac.

Jennings and his men rushed after him. Mireles, Cody, and the Rio Kid fanned out in the circular space deep in the canyon.

"Throw down, outlaws!" bawled the Rio Kid.

The shrill, blood-curdling Rebel yell rose from the throats of Jennings and his compatriots. It sent chills through the startled killers' hearts. They were rousing, trying to throw off their blankets and seize their arms.

Shots began banging, echoing in the canyon. The light was rapidly increasing, and in the drifting mists they could see well enough to operate. The Rio Kid jumped toward the spot where he had last seen George Hansinger. Drew Young, snarling, a Colt in hand, loomed before him. Both men fired at the same instant, the heavy guns booming pointblank.

154

The Rio Kid felt a paralyzing burn in his left leg. It shocked him so that he went down on his knee, saving himself by throwing out a hand. But Drew Young was falling backward. He struck a rock and fell dead, with the Rio Kid's bullet through his traitor brain.

"There's Hansinger! Watch it, Rio Kid!"

Buffalo Bill swerved, to send a hasty shot at George Hansinger. Hansinger had suddenly appeared from the side of a great boulder, and was upon the Rio Kid. His eyes glowed red as he cursed his archenemy. He had a shotgun in his hands, and was swinging to fill the Rio Kid with buck when Cody fired.

Hansinger whirled around, and the load of buckshot whooshed in the air over the Rio Kid's bent head. Pryor pulled himself together. He wanted Hansinger more than anything—not alive, either. He steadied himself.

His carbine had fallen to the ground, but a Colt was in his right hand. His thumb rose off the hammer spur.

"Let's see yuh get bail and wriggle out of this!" he muttered.

There was a dazed look on Hansinger's bearded face; his chin stuck out, farther and farther; his eyes were widening. His arms went down, and the shotgun clanked in the rocks. A small, but enlarging blotch showed in his forehead.

All about raged the quick fight, as Jennings and his hard-fighting cowmen overcame the camp. But the Rio Kid was staring at Hansinger as the Boss of Cheyenne slid from the side of the boulder and crumpled in the shale.

THE SUN was warm and yellow over the cow camp of the Texans. The Rio Kid lay on a blanket, his wound dressed by Sara Jennings and Alyse. Hot coffee and a meal had helped, and so had the nap he had taken. They had brought him straight to camp after the fight at the canyon, while the main party had remained, cleaning up, securing the captives.

Jennings, Cody and the others were bringing in trussed prisoners, outlaws of Cheyenne caught with Hansinger in the wild mountain gorge. Hands tied to saddle-horns, roped in bunches on their mustangs, the sullen-eyed desperadoes had come to the end of their tether.

Gus Jennings came over to see how the Rio Kid was doing. He mopped the dust and sweat from his red face and grinned down at Bob Pryor.

"Yuh all right?" he asked.

"Fine! Yuh wiped 'em up, I see."

"That's right, thanks to you. We buried Young, Hansinger and a couple more in the rocks. All we got was a few scratches and flesh wounds."

A drink was in order. Alyse and her mother brought liquor, cooled in jugs in the mountain stream. Frank Warren, Gus Jennings and his cronies, with Buffalo Bill Cody and Celestino Mireles clustered about to drink a toast to the Rio Kid. Cass Halpers, Dodge's engineer, joined in. He had been talking with Pryor earlier.

"You boys got plenty to be happy about, Jennings," agreed the Rio Kid. "Halpers says there's evidently big gas wells in this section. I overheard Hansinger and Drew Young talkin' of it last night. Hansinger had found out that Cheyenne plans to install gas lightin', mebbe even cook stoves! These wells are nearest to town, and worth a fortune!"

"Cook with gas!" gasped Mrs. Jennings. "Imagine thinking of such a thing! Why, wouldn't it blow you skyhigh?"

"Not if it's worked right," replied the Rio Kid. "It makes better light than oil, and is easier to handle. From what Hansinger said, Young had told him there was gas here, and Hansinger had decided he'd take over, so's he could really clean up before he lit out. That's why Hansinger was so dead-set on wipin' you fellers off the map. He wanted Warren out of the way, of course, but he thought he'd jump yore claims and get the wells."

Frank Warren nodded. "That's right. Tate advocated gas for Cheyenne, and I know they were going to see about it. It's worth a great deal."

They drank to victory, and to their luck. . . .

It was two days later when the Rio Kid, Buffalo Bill and Celestino said good-by to their

157

friends, the Texans. The prisoners had been sent to Cheyenne to the lockup.

General Dodge would see to their punishment.

Frank Warren stood with an arm around Alyse Jennings. He had told the Rio Kid that he was going to marry Alyse, and they would live in Cheyenne. Gus Jennings insisted he was going to buy a newspaper, and that Warren would run it.

The Rio Kid shook hands with the hearty Jennings and the other men in the cow camp. They were going to settle now on their respective sections, and with the proceeds of the gas wells, they would build to the sky.

Pryor limped a bit as he walked to his horse. It was a reminder of the savage fight at the canyon, when he had downed Drew Young and George Hansinger.

But it took more than a stiff leg to stop the Rio Kid. He mounted, sat his saddle, with Cody and the Mexican at either side. They swung off, waving to the Texans to whom Wyoming now was home. The Rio Kid uttered a glad war whoop, happy to be in the saddle again, riding the danger trails of the frontier.

Tom Curry was born in Hartford, Connecticut and graduated from college with a degree in chemical engineering. Leo Margulies, editorial director for N. L. Pines's Standard Magazines, encouraged Tom to write Western stories. In 1936, Margulies launched a new magazine titled *Texas Rangers*. Leslie Scott wrote the first several of these 45,000-word novelettes about Texas Ranger Jim Hatfield, known as the Lone Wolf, published under the house name Jackson Cole. Tom Curry's first Jim Hatfield story was "Death Rides the Rio" in *Texas Rangers* (3/37) and over the succeeding years he contributed over fifty Hatfield tales to this magazine alone. Curry also wrote three of the series novelettes for *Masked Rider Western* and some for *Range Riders Western*. It was in 1938 that Margulies asked Curry to devise a new Western hero for a pulp magazine and Tom came up with Bob Pryor. *The Rio Kid Western* published its first issue in October 1939. Subsequently Curry expanded several of his Rio Kid stories to form novels, published by Arcadia House, with the hero's name changed from Bob Pryor to Captain Mesquite. Possibly Curry's best Western fiction came during the decade of the 1940s, especially in the Jim Hatfield stories and in his Rio Kid novelettes. After Margulies was released from Standard Magazines, Curry quit writing and began a new career in 1951 with Door-Oliver, Inc., that lasted for fourteen years, working in their research and testing laboratory in Westport as accountant, purchasing agent, and customer service representative, making use at last of his chemical engineering degree. When Curry retired from Door-Oliver, he resumed writing Westerns sporadically for Tower Books and Pyramid Books and, later still, for Leisure Books. In October 1969, Margulies informed Curry that he was to be publishing a new digest-sized publication to be titled *Zane Grey Western Magazine* and he wanted Tom to write some new stories to appear in its pages featuring a number of Zane Grey's best known characters. These stories would be published under the house name Romer Zane Grey. Curry put a lot of talent and energy into so many of his Western novelettes, particularly the Rio Kid adventures, and his stories can still intrigue and entertain.